Whispers Through Water

Rebecca Wenrich Wheeler

*for my mom
and to the girls who went away, may someone tell your stories.*

Copyright © 2022 by Rebecca Wenrich Wheeler

All rights reserved.

Names, characters, places, and incidents are the product of the author's imagination. Any resemblance to actual events, locations, or persons, living or dead, is purely coincidental and not intentional unless otherwise stated.

Publisher: Monarch Educational Services, LLC

Original Art/Section Illustrations: Terri Moore

Developmental Editor by Kelly Martin; Line edits by Haley Hwang

Cover Design - Monarch Educational Services; Licensed Adobe Stock Photo

All rights reserved. No part of this book may be reproduced in any form or by any electronic or mechanical means, including information storage and retrieval systems, without written permission from the publisher, except for the use of brief quotations in a book review. Thank you for respecting the work of authors. www.monarcheducationalservices.com

1
GRAPE JUICE

Truth has rough flavours if we bite it through. — George Eliot

I drove the toe of my Doc Martens into the pile of the living room carpet and twisted my foot to make an indention. I don't know what angered me more—my aunt's harsh words, or that I let her get to me. I fiddled with the large safety pin that adorned my plaid miniskirt, repressing the urge to stab something with it.

"Young ladies look adults in the eye," Aunt Delia said, her voice wrapped in confidence. She shifted in her chair and crossed her legs.

"So, what exactly do you want me to say?" I asked, tilting my head toward the ceiling, hoping the tears would somehow drain back into my body.

I wiped my eyes, smearing blue mascara across the back of my hand, and squeezed the disintegrating tissue. "If you had these ridiculous restrictions on my college education, you should have told me earlier. My God, Aunt Delia, it's already April!"

I clenched my fists until I could feel my veins pulse. The tissue bits, wet with perspiration and mucus, stuck to the ridges in my palm.

"Ridiculous?" My aunt lowered her chin and peered at me over the rim of her glasses. Her small frame was deceptive. Aunt Delia's inner lioness pounced when it came to maintaining her order. "Gwyn, it's my money to give, and it's my money to take away. My house, my rules."

"Rules, what rules?" I made eye contact with my mom, who stood in the archway separating the living room and the staircase. "Mom, are you hearing this?"

Mom turned away. The dizziness of frustration traveled through my body.

I choked back tears. "Aunt Delia, you told me my whole life that you would pay for my college tuition, that you wanted me to earn a degree. I thought I only needed to get accepted. Why are you changing this on me now?"

"I expected you to attend college here"—she tapped her finger on the coffee table for emphasis—"in Virginia. Besides, you already accepted your admittance into William and Mary."

"Aunt Delia, the letter arrived today that I was off the waitlist. It's my number one choice. I am going to call and rescind my acceptance to William and Mary this week."

"I'm not sure why you would give up your seat, so many students would love the chance to go there. Plus, it's only thirty minutes away. You could even commute."

Aunt Delia folded the Massachusetts College of Art and Design acceptance letter dated April 1, 1998, and handed it to me as if it was just another grocery store flier.

"If only being thirty minutes away was the expectation," I said, "then you should have told me a heck of a lot earlier. If I was told, I wouldn't have even applied out of state, and I could have avoided getting my hopes up." I tugged on my black T-shirt, my torso damp with perspiration.

"Honestly, Gwyn, I never imagined there would be a need for this conversation."

"Why not?"

"Because I didn't expect you to get in." Aunt Delia's words were deliberate and icily calm.

I pressed my palm against my chest. Her words winded me, as if, instead of catching a basketball, it had hit me square in the gut. I couldn't tell if those were my aunt's actual feelings, or if she had just demeaned my intelligence to end the argument. I was out of comebacks. I turned, hoping to find empathy from my mom, but she had already left the room.

My aunt adjusted the collar of her blouse. She picked up a magazine from the coffee table and opened it with a snap. The April issue of *Southern Living* magazine was my cue. Aunt Delia was done with me.

MOM RINSED green grapes and set the strainer on a plate in the middle of the counter next to a tray of chocolate chip cookies and a bowl of sweet yogurt dip. She picked up a grape, swirled it in the dip, and popped it in her mouth. My mother ate when she was anxious, but somehow, she still managed to stay a size six.

She held out a cookie, but I waved away her offer. My stomach was still recovering from Aunt Delia's blow.

"It's like she makes up these crazy rules to shield her from reality or something, but the reality is, I've grown up." I pulled a paper napkin from its holder and dug grooves into the fibers until the napkin finally ripped. "This whole freaking thing, Mom. It's not fair."

"I know it feels cruel, but it's her way of trying to protect you, to keep you safe." Mom turned away, but if she wanted to keep me from seeing her quivering lip, she failed. She tried not to take sides, but I knew, deep down, she understood.

"You make it sound like we're living in the 1950s. Girls are capable of taking care of themselves." I drew a grape from the strainer and pressed lightly, making one end of the fruit bulge. "I am going to Boston. I'll figure out a way to convince her. You'll see."

Mom nodded in response, clicking her fingernails as she absentmindedly tapped the side of the metal strainer. The R.E.M. concert T-shirt Mom wore, which she took from a basket of my clean laundry, was pulled tight over her chest. I glanced down at my chest, so small that I had a clear view of my feet.

Mom and I existed more as good friends sharing the same roof rather than mother and daughter. My parents were married when they were nineteen, the stereotypical high school sweethearts. Their relationship exuded with passion, both in conflict and romance. I was born a year later, and my father left when I was two. Though, to my dad's credit, he showed up in unexpected ways.

After Dad left, Aunt Delia and Uncle Beckett came to our rescue; in truth, they were the ones who raised me. My mom, thirteen years younger than her sister, knew little of rearing a child. Aunt Delia's parents, my grandparents, gave her a lot of responsibility to care for her little sister. I think Aunt Delia thought of her sister more as a daughter. My mom started working night shifts soon after we moved in, and Aunt Delia took care of me. She prepared my meals, got me ready for school, and kept order. I had always known what to expect from her-but today, she blindsided me.

Tears surfaced again, and I tried to blink them back. Affixed to the refrigerator with a *Jesus Is Love* magnet was Aunt Delia's newspaper photo. She had gotten an award for her work with the town's annual Holiday Charity Auction. Even when Aunt Delia was given an award, she maintained a serious expression, no smile, but excellent posture.

"Mom, why didn't you stand up for me back there?" I pointed in the direction of the living room. Who was I kidding? This was my mother, the woman who named me Gwyneth after her favorite character from a 1980s soap opera.

She reached out to touch my hand, but I jerked it from the counter.

"You know how difficult your aunt is. Nothing I could have said would have made a difference."

"But I'm your daughter. You're supposed to take my side." The heat rose in my cheeks.

"And you know why I can't confront her," she said, her voice increasing in intensity. "It's your aunt's money, not mine."

The government said my mom made too much money as a hospital receptionist to award a decent amount of financial aid, but they haven't seen her savings account—that was, if she had one. My minimum-wage after-school job didn't leave much to save either. I loved my job at the florist, but after paying for car insurance and gas, it wouldn't cover two weeks of tuition.

"It's not like she would even have any money if she hadn't married Uncle Beckett." If my mother noticed the sarcasm in my voice, she didn't acknowledge it.

Mom slid off the kitchen stool and left me stewing at the counter.

I picked up the spoon from the bowl of fruit dip and used it as a catapult. I launched a grape, which bounced off the refrigerator underneath the newspaper photograph and landed on the floor. A blob of yogurt traveled down the side of the black refrigerator, the white streak became smaller and smaller before disappearing completely.

I SLEPT VERY little that night. I awoke every hour, my bedroom haunted by the green numbers of my digital alarm clock. By 5am, frustrated with my inability to sleep, I pushed aside my sheets and coaxed my legs off the side of the bed. My head throbbed. The horrible argument had crept into my dreams. As if in some Freudian nightmare, I found myself physically shrinking in front of my aunt as she grew in height, eventually breaking the living room ceiling with her head.

My aunt needed time to cool off, and I needed time to think. Engaging her in a constant battle would only make things worse. She wasn't the type of woman you could wear down.

My June graduation already loomed like a vulture over roadkill. I decided to make one last-ditch effort to convince her that my future lay elsewhere. I spent the weekend methodically rehearsing my appeal, writing and rewriting every detail. Once my fingernails were chewed into ragged oblivion and my Siamese cat, Cher, had begun to avoid me, I knew it was now or never. Either Aunt Delia would pay my tuition, or I would be bound to college loans, and I'd learn to live with that.

2
HEIRLOOMS

Monday morning, I slid out of bed, my body aching from a restless sleep. I studied my dark circles under my blue eyes in the bathroom mirror and pressed on my cheeks to bring some color to my face. I repeated "I am calm" to myself in the mirror, just like my school counselor had coached me to do. If Aunt Delia caught a glimpse of my anxiety, I wouldn't stand a chance. She did not tolerate weakness. My aunt's adoration for my best friend Denise Prescott baffled me, because Denise was wild. No one could resist Denise's self-assurance, not even Aunt Delia. Denise never became emotional in a conflict, unlike me, who cracked under pressure. In biology class junior year, I knew my answer to the mitochondria question was falsely marked incorrect, but I took the 95 instead of working up the nerve to confront my teacher. Maybe if it was a difference between an A or B, I would have garnered the will to ask for a grade change. When faced with conflict, silence was my default, and to override the default, the problem had to be life-altering. Aunt Delia had already witnessed my breaking point, so I had nothing more to lose. She would be more likely to listen if we met on her territory, where she was comfortable, maybe just enough to let her guard down.

Mom and I rarely set foot in Delia's office, which was really a small formal living room she converted into her office and was the one room in the house with a bay window. As a child, I always wanted to sit in the smooth window seat, but Aunt Delia used that space for her antique cobalt blue Depression glassware. I was always too terrified to move the colored vases and candlesticks.

After Aunt Delia and Uncle Beckett were married, she attended community college and completed an associate degree in accounting. She became the bookkeeper at my uncle's bookstore, the local daycare, and a hardware store. Aunt Delia valued hard work. A large rolltop desk faced the wall to the left of the bay window, but instead of calling it a desk, she used the formal name: a secretary. Pictures of pressed flowers in classic wooden frames hung in a precise formation on the opposite wall, and a picture of Uncle Beckett holding me as a baby sat on top of her desk. The gentle clinking of the spoon against the sides of a teacup echoed in an otherwise silent room. She sat at her desk with her back to the door. A film of white light enveloped the room, as the afternoon sun fought its way into the space.

An elastic bubble rose in my esophagus. I winced and mumbled, *Oh, God*, partly out of fear, and partly out of prayer. I tapped lightly on the smooth inner surface of the archway with my knuckles.

Aunt Delia turned in her chair toward me and tilted her chin downward to look at me over the rim of her glasses. She held a teacup in her right hand. "Come over here, dear. Your mother said you wanted to talk to me."

My right-hand clenched as I took two steps forward. The slow creak of the hardwood floor amplified with each step.

"Yes, I wanted to talk to you." I hesitated, fully aware of Aunt Delia's knowing stare. I swallowed audibly. "I wanted to talk to you about college again."

"I think we have exhausted that topic, haven't we?" She stirred her tea with her favorite little spoon, decorated with a British flag, a souvenir from Uncle Beckett's time in London after graduate school.

"Yes, almost, but I thought we could, like, figure out a compromise." I glanced at my aunt's feet, clad in navy ballet flats that served as her slippers. For as long as I can remember, I've never seen her without shoes. "And I didn't mean to be so angry last time we talked. I'm calmer now."

"I appreciate that, but if we are going to have this little discussion, you must step closer. I won't bite. I haven't in a long time." Aunt Delia smiled at her own joke.

I almost said, "I know," and rolled my eyes, but I held back my sarcasm. My aunt claimed I inherited sarcasm from my dad, and she hated anything that had to do with him. If she looked at me and was reminded of Dad, that would not help my case. As I moved toward the cherry wood tea table, a light breeze caught the sheer curtains causing them to balloon and deflate. Maybe the curtains trembled in Aunt Delia's presence too.

I released my clinched fist. "Aunt Delia, I know you want what's best for me, and I feel what's best for me is to go to Boston. My mind is made up."

"Okay."

I inhaled sharply waiting for her retort that never came. When she gave no further response, I continued, "My art teacher is very excited. Around here, not many students leave the state for college."

At the word *art*, Aunt Delia's eyes dropped to her lap, and her slender fingers smoothed her dress. After a moment's pause, she stared directly at me, her forehead creased heavy in thought. My mother told me my blue eyes grew more vibrant when I became emotional. I hoped my eyes did not give me away now.

"I agree that being accepted is an accomplishment. But I can't see sending my small-town seventeen-year-old niece hours away to study art."

"It's graphic design, Aunt Delia. My major is graphic design."

Aunt Delia tilted her head as if asking a question without speaking.

"You know, using computers." I pretended to type on an invisible computer. My aunt grunted, but her face would never have given that away. "I'll be eighteen once the semester begins. I know I'm mature enough to handle this."

"And you're here asking me to reconsider paying your tuition."

I nodded my head sheepishly. The script I carefully practiced in the bathroom now seemed irrelevant. Suddenly fidgety, I shifted my weight to my right foot. Looking down, I noticed a torn Chiquita banana sticker had fused itself to the toe of my shoe. The dancer on the sticker even seemed to scowl at me.

"I have received a partial scholarship and a little financial aid, so you wouldn't be paying the full amount." My body sagged.

"I won't stop you from leaving, but if you do, you know my answer." Aunt Delia took a sip of tea and placed the cup on the saucer without making a sound. "You're on your own."

Her words, while sharp, only prompted a sigh. Even surrounded by people, I've always felt as if I was on my own.

"I've already sent in the enrollment deposit with my own money. My decision is made."

"Well then, I think we're done here, Gwyn."

"Yes, ma'am." I shrugged and pressed my fingertips to my temple, massaging my head in a circular motion.

"Just so we understand one another." She glanced at the grandfather clock. "My, how time flies. Four-thirty already. If you would excuse me, I need to begin dinner."

She gathered the tea service and the magazine she had been reading when I interrupted her. Defeated, I slumped toward the archway of the living room. Before leaving, I turned and met my aunt's steadfast gaze.

"Aunt Delia, when you were young, didn't you want to break out and see the world? To leave your small town?"

"No, Gwyn, I didn't have the luxury."

I decided not to mention art, Boston, loans, degrees, trains, or anything that had to do with college or travel in the presence of Aunt Delia. The last two months of my senior year had enough to worry about between AP exams and prom.

When I didn't have a date to prom, my mom set me up with Will Turnbull, the son of her co-worker. She said, "He will make a good picture," which was all the justification Mom needed.

Will was much more into me than I was into him, so an hour into prom after I wasn't reciprocating his affection, he decided to leave with Miranda Peoples and her very short dress. I ended up riding home with Danny and Denise, the third-wheel saviors.

I managed to go two months without another argument with Aunt Delia. She talked about William and Mary, and I nodded without comment, even when she gave me a green-and-gold college sweatshirt on my last day of school. While my aunt thought she had convinced me to stay, I had already submitted my acceptance. To pay the initial tuition deposit, I combined the money I saved from my after-school job with the sale of one of my dad's vintage guitars. Dad had given it to Mom the second time he tried to win her back. Mom said she waited to sell the guitar for something important.

I figured I still had the summer to win Aunt Delia over, but my hope died suddenly. I had forgotten that after each graduate received their diploma, the principal announced their intended future plans, whether that was college, military, or a trade school.

My heartbeat accelerated with each letter of the alphabet. I prayed that the microphone would somehow malfunction when the assistant principal made it to the M's, but a miracle glitch did not occur. Principal Swinton wiped his hand on his graduation robe after shaking my sweaty palm. Then Assistant Principal Balmer bellowed in her Midwestern accent, "Gwyneth Luanne Madison, Magna Cum Laude, Massachusetts College of Art and Design."

Through the applause and cheers, I swear I heard my Aunt Delia's distinctive gasp. After graduation, Denise and I shared a party at her house. My aunt spoke to everyone in attendance but managed to avoid me the entire night.

3
UNCLE BECKETT

We sat in silence at the breakfast table the morning after graduation. I found it ridiculous that Aunt Delia insisted we eat together on Saturday mornings, especially during the summer. At least she allowed the family to eat at the informal dining table in the kitchen. Uncle Beckett always sat at an angle facing the kitchen window, most likely to separate him from any ensuing women's debates. He propped his right ankle on his left knee and read the editorials.

Aunt Delia drank coffee only in the morning. I often fantasized about sneaking a spoonful of Jack Daniels in her cup. She did not know Uncle Beckett hid a bottle in his office behind a rare edition of *The Rime of the Ancient Mariner*. My mom worked at the hospital five nights a week, eight at night to four in the morning; she was the only family member Aunt Delia allowed to miss breakfast.

I studied the Cheerios in my bowl, pressing each circle with my spoon and watching them bounce back to the milk's surface. I imagined myself as a soggy and expanding Cheerio drowning in milk. Uncle Beckett patted me on the knee with his hand, the one hidden by the newspaper. In the morning he smelled of spearmint from his favorite shaving cream. He never cared for wearing a beard like other men of his generation.

"Gwynnie, I'll take you to work today," Uncle Beckett said

before taking the last sip of his coffee. "I want to talk to you anyway."

"Thanks, Uncle Beck." I smiled at him. Uncle's bookshop was three blocks from my job at the florist where I worked for the past two years. I mainly answered the phone and took orders, but I enjoyed being surrounded by beauty every day, second only to being away from the house.

Aunt Delia remained silent. She ate her grapefruit and yogurt as if it were an occupation, trying to avoid making direct eye contact with me.

"Aunt Delia, if you are finished with your dishes, I'll take it to the sink for you," I said, more out of a reason to leave the table than to be nice.

"No, thank you, Gwyn, I am not quite finished."

I glanced at her plate. Only a small puddle of grapefruit juice remained. That would be so like her, drinking the last bit of sour fluid just to spite me.

"You can take mine." Uncle Beckett winked and handed me his plate.

"Of course."

I placed the dishes in the sink. Instead of taking the stairs to my bedroom, I stood with my back against the living room wall in order to peer into the kitchen without being seen.

Uncle Beckett neatly folded his newspaper and laid it on the placemat. He stood and looked at his wife. She continued to stare straight ahead at the pantry door.

"You need to go easy on that girl, Delia. She's all we have." He tapped the wooden table twice with his fingers and exited through the back door. After Uncle Beckett left the room, Aunt Delia picked up her plate and carried it to the sink.

Angry, I ran up the stairs to my room. I do not know if Aunt Delia ever heard me.

"It's not my money, Gwyn," Uncle Beckett said as he drove down Riverbend's main street.

I shivered, as if startled from a daydream. "What?"

"It's not my money to give. I wanted you to know that." Uncle Beckett kept his eyes fixed on the road ahead.

"I'm sorry. I was really mad when I told mom that Aunt Delia only married you for your money. It was stupid. I didn't even know she heard me, and I didn't mean to offend you."

"No, Gwynnie, you couldn't offend me." Beckett glanced down at my electric blue fingernails and leather bracelet fashioned with metal grommets. "Well, maybe." Uncle Beckett laughed, and I shoved my hands under my legs.

"So, can you tell me?" I asked.

"Where the money came from?" Uncle Beckett sighed.

"Yeah, that's what I meant."

"I'm sorry, sweetheart, but that's not my story to tell."

I knew I should not press my uncle any further. He had told me more personal information in the last four minutes than he had my entire life. To me, Uncle Beckett had always been the man who snuck his niece cookies before dinner and let the dog, Pepper, in the house when Aunt Delia wasn't at home. Of course, when we heard her Chrysler approaching, we had to quickly push Pepper out the back door and clean the brown mess she would inevitably leave on the linoleum. Uncle Beckett had always been my refuge when life got too serious.

"Here we are. Don't roll your eyes when you answer the phone."

"Uncle," I whined in my best five-year-old voice.

"See." Uncle Beckett waved his pointer finger at me.

"What is it with old people and that finger?" I smiled and kissed him on the cheek.

"I'll be in the bookshop if you need anything," Uncle Beckett called to me through the open passenger window. He shifted the car into gear and drove the few blocks to the bookshop he had owned for over thirty years.

The shopkeeper's bell signaled my arrival, prompting Mrs. Jenkins, the owner of The Fragrant Garden, to emerge from the back room.

"Hello, Gwyn; right on time, as usual." She grinned, her yellow shirt as bright as the vase of lilies she carried. She placed the vase in the cooler where we kept the ready-made bouquets.

Mrs. Jenkins had to be one of the most pleasant people I knew. She once told me that her purpose was to make the difficult times easier to take and the joyous times more memorable. She asked me to design business cards with her motto, but I told her there wouldn't be enough room. She finally settled for "flowers designed with love".

Mrs. Jenkins was the first African American woman to own a business in our small town. I'd met her when she'd spoken to my business class my sophomore year on incorporating art and entrepreneurship. Mrs. Jenkins' excitement inspired me so much, I asked her for a job that day.

"I will be in the back working on the flowers for the McCormick wedding. Would you mind designing the newspaper ad? You are so good at that." Mrs. Jenkins smiled and patted me on the shoulder.

"No problem. Anything else?"

"Oh yes, Lee Graves. I always thought that was a horrible name for a funeral director— anyway, he is coming to pick those up this morning." Mrs. Jenkins pointed to two large arrangements of yellow and white lilies.

She picked up a pair of scissors and a new spool of purple satin ribbon. She twirled the spool around her finger as she glided to the back room.

I scanned the shop looking for flowers to sketch. The left side of the refrigerated case held vases of roses, red and vibrant. Typically, men purchased these bouquets ten minutes before the store closed because they forgot their wife's birthday or the couple's anniversary. The slogan "we save your butt" might be more fitting for the newspaper advertisement. I could imagine Aunt Delia's eyes bulging from her head when she read it, especially if she knew I produced the impropriety.

My eyes fell on the arrangement of lilies, which appeared to grow larger the longer I stared. I had always thought of lilies as funeral flowers. I had first seen them cascading from acrylic baskets on either side of my grandmother's coffin, and I've hated lilies ever since.

My grandmother died when I was five, and my grandpa three

months later. I heard that it was common for spouses who had been married a long time to die close together. My aunt asserted that it was not appropriate for a five-year-old girl to attend a funeral, but I wanted to go. I needed to be with my mom. Aunt Delia and Mom fiercely argued about my attendance, but Aunt Delia won; after all, we were living in her house.

The funeral began at eleven in the morning. Aunt Delia instructed me to stay in the church basement helping the hospitality committee prepare for the reception. Eventually, the church ladies became so engrossed in gossip, they forgot about me so I made my escape.

Grandmother's church always had confused me. The catacomb of hallways all seemed the same; each wall adorned with monochromatic pictures of the apostles in cheap frames. The floor creaked, so I took off my shoes and tiptoed through the endless maze of crimson carpet. I noticed my big toe had freed itself through a hole in my tights.

I followed the voice of Mrs. Mulligan singing "Jesus Savior Pilot Me," every verse becoming louder as I neared the sanctuary. It did not cross my mind that the voice would be loudest at the front of the sanctuary—near the altar, and my grandmother's casket. It also did not occur to me that I should have made my escape outside and entered through the vestibule.

Following the voice's lead, I opened the door and stepped through. Mrs. Mulligan stopped singing, and all eyes turned to look at me standing in the choir loft.

For Grandpa's funeral, I was left at my dad's house, two counties away.

4
DOODLES

Uncle Beckett liked to keep the house cold in the summer, so despite it being June, I kept a fleece blanket on my bed year-round. I held the phone receiver to my ear with my elbow propped on a pillow.

"Do you want me to have a talk with her? I think I would make a good defense attorney." I pictured Denise fingering her hoop earrings as she spoke.

I had never seen Denise without large hoop earrings. In physical appearance, we could not be more different. Denise stood at a petite five-foot-three, with naturally sleek black hair, which she maintained in a short trendy cut. Denise exuded grace with a lovable edge. I, on the other hand, often felt awkward, never knowing where to position my uncoordinated long limbs or how to quite style my wavy brunette hair that fell several inches below my shoulders.

"I'm not in the mood for jokes right now," I said.

"Oh, you know I love your family, even Aunt Delia." Denise laughed. "I think she might like me more than you!"

"I don't doubt that."

I met Denise in the third grade when we bonded over Garbage Pail Kids trading cards, which were considered contraband in both of our homes. I loved Denise for her sense of adventure, but when it came to topics of a serious nature, she had a difficult time staying focused.

"God, Gwyn, you don't know how lucky you are. You have a free ticket out of this town."

"It's not free, Denise. I still have to figure out how to pay for it."

"I'm not talking about money. You have an adventure waiting for you in Boston, while I'm stuck here going to community college with the losers who couldn't get through algebra."

"It's not my fault you waited until April to apply for colleges."

"Lighten up, Gwyn. I thought we were talking about your problems."

"Sorry, that wasn't fair of me. I know you had other things on your mind."

Denise's dad spent several weeks in the hospital after a construction accident at the beginning of our senior year. He was home by Halloween, but it took her a while to get her focus back, and she missed the fall application deadlines.

"You're forgiven." Denise sighed.

"Thanks." I could almost feel Denise poking me to let me know we were okay.

"Back to your problem. I think you should just go to Boston, take out loans, and don't look back."

"It's not that easy. This is my family." I swirled a pencil on my notebook. The light from the fluorescent desk lamp illuminated a picture of me and Uncle Beckett behind glass in a plain purple frame.

"Look, your mom and Uncle Beck will always support you, and for your Aunt Delia, I think she'll come to terms with it eventually. You know, like, ten years from now."

"No kidding. I'm afraid when I leave, I won't be welcome to come home again." I rubbed the edges of the frame and passed my thumb over my uncle's face.

"Just the price you have to pay for success," Denise responded with a trill in her voice.

"Whatever, Denise."

"I'm sorry. I'll stop joking around. I guess I'm a little jealous."

"Why?"

"I'm jealous that you have a choice."

I sighed. "I didn't think of it that way."

"Follow what your heart is telling you."

"I'll have to make it through the summer. Do you think Mrs. Jenkins will let me set up a cot at the shop?"

"Sleeping with all those plants would be creepy. Like that '80s musical my mom made me watch. What was the title?" She clicked her tongue. "*Little Shop of Horrors.*"

I rolled my eyes as if she could see me. "Okay, so you won't be visiting me. I don't know, maybe my goal should be to make Aunt Delia's life a little more miserable, just like she did mine."

"I'm sure that won't be a problem. Though I know whatever you decide, you will have thought through every possible angle."

"I do tend to overthink things."

"You're just realizing this fact?" She laughed. "I still love you though."

"Thanks for listening, Denise."

I tapped my pencil eraser, making a soft *thump, thump*. I did have a choice, and there was satisfaction in that.

I returned the phone receiver to its base and fiddled with the pencil. A large heart with the word *Boston* filled the top half of the lined paper. I added an arrow piercing the heart. The tip of the arrow contained Aunt Delia's face with the hair of Medusa. My own words, "Make your aunt's life a little more miserable," played like a scratched cassette tape in my mind until the mental noise became hazy static.

I balled up the notebook paper and aimed a throw at the metal wastebasket by my bedroom door. I missed hitting my sleeping cat snuggling in a basket of dirty laundry. Cher released a squeal and leapt. In her wake, she flung dirty socks across the floor with her hind legs.

The dusk settled in the June sky through my second story window. I rested my hands on my forehead, elbows propped on either side of the notebook. My eyes fell on a second doodle, one I must have inadvertently drawn during my phone call with Denise. In big block letters *not my story* glared back at me.

"Uncle Beckett, what are you trying to tell me?" I said aloud. There had always been something about my aunt that made me think more bubbled underneath her tough-as-nails exterior. Sometimes I noticed a fleeting sadness in her eyes, but she never held it long enough for anyone to be sure. A story lay underneath the money; I was sure of it.

I turned off the desk lamp, casting a shadow on my uncle's face in the photograph. I decided not to throw away that particular page.

A KNOCK JARRED me out of my inner thoughts. I turned to find Mom standing in my open doorway. She always knocked whether my bedroom door was open or not. My mom prided herself on respecting my privacy, not wanting to be a *typical* mom; those were her words.

She reached down and picked up my misdirected ball of notebook paper and dropped it in the trash can. "Cher's in a bad mood," Mom said. "She bolted past me on the stairs and hissed."

"That's my fault. I missed the trashcan and hit her with a ball of paper."

"Athletics were never your strong suit." Mom smiled, trying to lighten my obvious poor humor. "I wanted to pop my head in and say goodnight before I left for the hospital."

My mom always aspired to become a nurse. She enrolled in the nursing program at the community college when I was in middle school, but she dropped out her second year. I had always hoped that after I went away to college, Mom would return to school.

After we moved in with Aunt Delia, my mom took a job at the hospital as a receptionist in the emergency room. She had earned a lot of respect from the staff for being thorough and responsible, and because she never took any crap from anyone. The doctors were impressed by how my mom handled the numerous inebriated individuals and ambulance-chasing lawyers that came through the door. It always baffled me that my mom was more comfortable confronting arrogant lawyers than my aunt.

"Mom, before you go, I wanted to ask you something." I turned in my chair to face the doorway. "How much older is Uncle Beckett than Aunt Delia?"

"Fourteen years."

"Wow, weird."

I imagined Aunt Delia as a Jane Austen protagonist. I could just see her, fully dressed in Victorian garb, being instructed to marry an older widower to secure the family's social status.

"They married when I was six, so I don't remember much about that time." Mom paused, her eyes reminiscent. "They went to Italy on their honeymoon. I still have the rosary beads they brought back for me. They were made of rose quartz; she knew pink was my favorite color."

Most people would bring a six-year-old a stuffed animal or a picture book, but of course we were talking about Aunt Delia.

"And they never had any kids of their own?"

"Nope, but as soon as you were born, Beckett was in love." Mom reached down and returned my stray dirty socks to the laundry basket. "You know, I've always thought that might be the cause of Delia's tension, like she's jealous."

"What do you mean?" Mom's suggestion dumbfounded me, but I enjoyed the idea that Aunt Delia wasn't perfect.

"Well, more jealous of your relationship with Uncle Beckett. He adores you and always has." Mom made direct eye contact with me. "That's one of the reasons I never left Riverbend; I couldn't take you away from him."

That and not knowing how to manage away from the security of this house, but I could not deny Uncle Beckett's fondness of me.

"I still don't get it. Why would she be jealous of me?" I asked.

"Delia was accustomed to being the center of attention, but that attention was taken away, first by me, and then by you. That's my theory anyway."

"I just wish she hadn't decided to take it out on me."

"Honey, if you are worried about the money, we'll figure something out."

"Thanks, Mom."

For the better part of the last ten years, Mom had been paying off loans and debts she and dad accrued during their short marriage. I hated to burden her. Aunt Delia liked to remind my mom that she wasted her college money on that man, meaning my dad. My mother's college money now sat in our driveway in the form of a nineteen-year-old white Corvette. Too bad the car's value didn't even equal a semester's worth of tuition.

After we moved in with Aunt Delia, all of her efforts were focused on making me the perfect, well-disciplined child. My aunt had made it clear from my childhood that she would be responsible for guiding and paying for my education.

"Don't stay up too late." Mom turned to leave as Cher waltzed back into the room and jumped on the bed. "Oh, it looks like she is speaking to you again."

Aunt Delia hated animals in the house, let alone animals sleeping on beds, but she made an exception for Cher. She was a gift from Uncle Beckett when my grandparents passed away. Not even Aunt Delia would deny a child the comfort of a pet. I knew Uncle Beckett would still let Cher have the run of the house after I went to Boston; I wasn't worried about that.

This summer I needed to save as much money as I could. I was leaving whether I had my aunt's blessing or not. Talking about the matter further wouldn't change that fact.

5
THE UPSTAIRS ROOM

I always believed that the bookstore was my uncle's means of speaking to the world, a world he left when he moved to Riverbend. I roamed the aisles of bookshelves, lightly brushing my fingers across spines of early editions of Franz Kafka, Emily Dickinson, and Langston Hughes, letting the embossed leather press humanity into my fingers. The bookshop had become a tourist destination, a stop on the drive to the coast. Few bookshops could boast such an extensive selection of rare finds. Uncle Beckett also sold new books, mainly popular fiction and biographies, in order to keep the locals interested.

I often spent my lunch break with my uncle. We didn't talk much, only briefly looking up from our melted cheese and tomato on whole wheat to wave off the possible customer who did not bother to read the *Closed for Lunch* sign on the glass door.

Ever since Uncle Beckett revealed that Aunt Delia's money had a story, his nervous habits seemed more pronounced. He rubbed the back of his neck with his right hand, pretending to calm a knot that had developed, and bounced his leg as he sat on the counter stool. Maybe he feared that he had said too much, or wished he knew how to say more.

"Before you go back to work, I have something I want to show you." Uncle Beckett wiped his mouth with a napkin and tossed it in the trash can. As per his usual post-lunch ritual, Uncle Beckett pulled out the small handheld mirror that he kept on the shelf under the cash register. He smiled wide to make sure no seeds or lettuce strands were stuck in his teeth. Then he pulled the black plastic comb from his shirt pocket and ran it through his salt and pepper hair. He always kept his hair short, but I imagined that grown out he would have coarse curls.

"Okay, I still have twenty minutes."

"It's upstairs." Uncle Beckett stood and unhooked a key from underneath the counter. "Leave your plate. I'll clean up later."

Uncle Beckett had lived in the room above the bookshop when he first came to town. After he married Aunt Delia, he moved to the house on Foxwood Road, where they had lived ever since. As a child, I imagined stories about the upstairs room being filled with secret treasure, or better yet, where Uncle Beckett hid his spy equipment—innocent bookshop owner by day, CIA agent by night. I had never entered the room, and a part of me wished to remain ignorant.

"Be careful; I never replaced the hand railing." Uncle Beckett pointed to a foot-long absence of handrail at the top of the stairs. He stopped in front of the antique door and blew off the dust that coated the brass doorknob.

"It's been about two years since I've been up here." He paused and twisted the key. "Hold your nose, it's going to be dusty."

Uncle Beckett opened the door and stepped over the threshold. I followed.

The long room covered the expanse of the bookshop below. Two dormer windows faced Main Street, and two pane windows faced the side street. A small bathroom consumed one corner to the left of the main door, and a kitchenette filled the space to the right of the bathroom. A Victorian couch with wooden clawed feet loomed in the middle of the room, covered in a layer of dust that barely exposed the worn green velvet seat cushion. An open-top cardboard box was positioned on the couch, with synthetic Christmas garland draped over the edge. Along the wall, the sides of wooden frames peeked out from underneath faded quilts.

"Have I told you that I lived in London for four years before moving here to Riverbend?"

"Uh huh." My eyes moved from ceiling plank to plank. The dust particles danced in the stream of light passing through the curtainless windows.

"Um, Uncle Beck, I never understood why you moved here, especially from London."

Uncle Beckett rubbed the back of his neck with his hand, his eyes settling on the bare light bulb fixed to a socket in the ceiling.

"Let's just say I went to England to find my footing," he said.

"Then how did you come to Riverbend? You had no family here."

Uncle Beckett kept his back to me and knelt beside the quilt-covered frames. "As a child, my family drove through Riverbend every summer on our way to the coast. We had a small vacation home about an hour from here. I thought Riverbend would be a good place for a fresh start."

"Do your parents still own the vacation home?"

"No, they sold it after—" Uncle Beckett pursed his lips as if to stop a word from being released. "They sold it right before you were born."

He picked up the frame closest to the wall and lifted it, freeing a corner of the quilt from the floor.

"Come, Gwynnie. This is what I wanted to show you."

He removed the first quilt to reveal six large canvases, then the second quilt to reveal six more, and then another five, and another four.

"You can touch them," he said to me quietly.

I stood in front of the first group and reverently peeled back the canvases one by one. They were all still lives of various subjects: grapes, chipped teacups, a corn-husk angel in a bed of pansies. The second stack of paintings consisted mostly of landscapes, primarily of the rivers surrounding our peninsula. Renderings of the turn-of-the-century homes along Main Street made up the third grouping, and the fourth were abstracts that seemed remarkably out of character for the artist. I thought the abstracts must have been the artist's way of screaming, something that could not be accomplished by painting fruit.

"These are beautiful, and the colors are so"—I paused searching for the right word to do the paintings justice—"vibrant."

I added, "Whose are these?"

Uncle Beckett took off his glasses and wiped them with his handkerchief. I made eye contact with him, hoping to encourage an answer.

"Your Aunt Delia's," he finally said.

I froze. I tried to imagine Aunt Delia in a painting smock, with a permanent smudge on her right middle finger. "No, be serious, Aunt Delia? *My* Aunt Delia? When did she do all of this?"

"High school." Uncle Beckett rubbed a cloth gently over one of the canvases to remove the excess dust. "With the exception of the abstracts, she did those later."

"High school? She was this talented in high school?"

"Don't act so surprised." Uncle Beckett's tone became more amused as our eyes met. "Just think what an artist you already are. A family gift."

"I am not this good. So why—why did she stop?"

"Life has other plans, you know. Back then, there weren't as many opportunities to pursue your dreams, especially for women." Uncle Beckett stood and straightened a stack of canvases. "Let's put the quilts back. We want to keep them protected."

As we covered the paintings, I thought about how many times Aunt Delia had lectured me on Women's Suffrage, and how I should appreciate my educational opportunities. I remember her telling me that women couldn't even get a credit card until 1974. My thoughts drifted to my mom and how she took nursing courses while taking care of me.

"I guess life does have other plans sometimes," I said, mostly so I could hear myself think.

Uncle Beckett lifted my chin to meet his eyes. "But that doesn't mean you should put off yours, Gwynnie, and I think deep down, Delia doesn't want you to, either."

I smiled.

"Okay, enough of this." Uncle Beckett dusted off his pants with his hands. "I need to get downstairs to re-open the shop."

I surveyed the room one last time and noticed a clear Christmas ornament lying under the dormer window next to a large trunk. The ornament was a perfect ball of glass with a red cardinal suspended in the middle. I dusted it off with my sleeve.

"You can keep that as a souvenir," Uncle Beckett said.

"Thanks."

"I'm actually surprised it hasn't been broken after all these years."

"Hey, Uncle, what's in this trunk?" I pointed to an antique steamer trunk with a vine of yellow roses painted down one side.

"It's your Aunt Delia's hope chest from when she was a girl. When you and Trish moved into our house, she moved some old stuff up here to make room. I never use this space anyway."

"What's a hope chest?"

"It's a tradition that's gone out of style. Parents used to give a chest to the oldest daughter. She collected special items in the trunk until she got married."

"Oh." I traced the painted vine with my finger. "Aren't you curious what's in there?"

"Not in the slightest. Some of us aren't as nosy as others." He touched the tip of my nose with his pointer finger. "It's a lady's thing anyway. I honestly never thought much about it."

"Are you sure? I could easily pop that lock open." I smiled jokingly.

"You wouldn't dare." Uncle Beckett chuckled. He motioned for me to walk downstairs first and then turned to lock the door before descending the wooden staircase and replacing the key to its hook under the counter. "Go change the sign on the door, Gwyn."

"Sure. Hey, Uncle." I hesitated at the door. "Why are you telling me all of this now—I mean about the money and the paintings?"

Uncle Beckett looked up from the counter, his brown eyes growing deeper. "Well, Gwynnie." He rubbed his palm against the stair rail. "There's more to Delia than appears on the surface. I know you two aren't on the best of terms right now. I just wanted you to understand her a bit better before you left. Family fights, but family can reconcile too. Maybe, one day, the thing you have in common will bring you together."

"You mean art."

"Yes, at least that's my hope."

I smiled, without words to respond. Maybe the sadness that occasionally slipped into Aunt Delia's eyes had something to do with the paintings. I hoped the price of becoming an adult wasn't letting go of your passions for what the world deemed the more appropriate choice. Work, discipline, decorum, that's all I knew my aunt to be. Maybe I was wrong, or maybe I only saw what she wanted me to see.

In the quiet of the moment, the gentle ticking of the clock amplified. Hanging above the bookcase of biographies, a silhouette of Shakespeare filled the center of the clockface. If I stared at old William long enough, his lips would rhythmically repeat *tick tock*. My uncle's gaze followed mine to land on the clock.

"Gwynnie, aren't you supposed to be at work in 10 minutes?"

"Oh," I said, my eyes darting quickly from the clock to my uncle and back. "Love you. I'll see you at home."

I waved, slammed the door behind me, and ran the three blocks to the florist, clutching the glass ornament so it wouldn't slip out of my hands.

6
THE LETTER

On Mondays, the florist shop closed at three o'clock. Normally, I would take my time returning home, stopping for a snow cone at the Ice Shack or hanging out with Denise at her job at the pharmacy. Since the beginning of June, however, my focus had been getting home in time to check the mail. I wanted to be the first one to put hands on my housing assignment.

Aunt Delia had a habit of going through my mail if she got to it first. The summer before my freshman year, I attended summer camp and met a boy from Maryland. It was one of those "yes, no, maybe, check here" romances. I checked "yes" in a note passed to me during a leather craft lesson. We spent two weeks staring at each other across the camp dining hall and sneaking to hold hands during campfire sing-a-longs. We stayed in touch long after going home. We wrote to each other through the remainder of the summer and into the fall semester of our freshman year—that is, until Aunt Delia discovered a card around Halloween.

"What's this?" She waved an envelope in the air and crossed her arms, holding the card between her index and middle fingers.

My eyes dropped to my toes. "Where did you find it?"

"On your bed. I saw it when I brought up your laundry."

"Oh," I said under my breath.

"Who's sending you cards?"

"It's just a friend."

"He signed it, *Luv, Brian.*" Aunt Delia drew out her words. She opened the card and pointed to the handwriting.

"I promise. It's just a friend from summer camp," I said, snatching the card from her hand only to have Aunt Delia snatch the card back from me. I conceded defeat.

"You are too young to receive letters from boys we do not know about."

From that time on, I gave out the bookshop address to boys at summer camp. Uncle Beckett never opened my mail, and Aunt Delia never went to the bookshop. It seemed to be a perfect solution. I only wished I had thought to put the bookshop address on my college applications. I knew she would stop a letter from a boy, but I never dreamed she would do the same for a college.

A CLOCK SHAPED like a sunflower hung above the florist door. The repetitive ticking of the clock only seemed to lengthen the last fifteen minutes of my shift. I fingered the crystal necklace Denise had given me. My best friend believed she could sense people's auras, and she told me the necklace would bring tranquility, something she claimed I needed desperately. I wore it because I liked how light refracted on the wall when I twirled the crystal.

"Hey, Gwyn," Mrs. Jenkins called from the back room.

"Yes, ma'am?"

"You can leave a few minutes early. Once I finish this order, I'm going to close up."

"Hey, thanks." I clapped with excitement. "I'll see you tomorrow."

After grabbing my burgundy corduroy purse, I ran to my car. I planned to meet our mail carrier as he pulled up to our mailbox at three-twenty, as I had done for the past two Mondays, hoping that my housing assignment would arrive on a day Aunt Delia did not reach the mailbox first.

I made the right turn to our street without slowing down and pulled into our driveway. The mail carrier rounded the corner as he moved from mailbox to mailbox. With one leg already hanging outside the driver's side door, I waited to pounce. As soon as he pulled up to our box, I approached him.

"Hello, Miss Madison. Rather excited about the mail?"

"Hey, Mr. Phillips, I— I've been waiting for something." I tried to sound cool and collected, but my pounding heart told me I was anything but.

"Well, here ya go." Mr. Phillips handed me a stack of envelopes and magazines through the window of the mail truck and tipped his cap. "You have a good day now."

"Thanks."

I gave Mr. Phillips a half wave and returned to my car. I sat with the door open, my legs stretched outside.

I leafed carefully through the mail. The electric bill, L.L. Bean catalog, credit card application, letter for Aunt Delia, and one addressed to me with *Massachusetts* in the return address.

"Yes!" I screamed aloud and beat my fist against the doorframe in jubilation.

I ripped open the letter in a fury, inadvertently tearing Aunt Delia's envelope as well. "Crap, she's going to kill me."

I realized that I had not only ripped her envelope, but a strip of the letter as well. I pulled the stationary out of the envelope to see if somehow I could tape the letter back together to make it look like the sender's accident. I held the ripped strip in one hand and unfolded the letter in the other.

I had no intention of reading the letter, but the sender's large script made the text difficult to ignore. The letter contained one sentence, which filled the top half of the nondescript tan stationary.

June 10, 1998

Delia,

Andrew was married last Saturday in Philadelphia.

*In peace,
Sr. Susan*

    I did not blink for several seconds. I repeated the words *Andrew was married* in a hushed whisper. *Philadelphia,* the city of brotherly love. My mind reeled. I knew of no one named "Andrew." In lieu of a return address, the sender had simply written *Sr. Susan* in the same neat script in the top left corner of the envelope. The only mark of the letter's origin was the recent Philadelphia postmark.

    Sweat formed on my skin, even my thumbs, which left two wet, limp ovals on either side of the letter. Feeling the ghost-like presence of Aunt Delia, I glanced over each shoulder to insure I was alone. I folded the mysterious letter, placed it in my purse, and gathered the rest of the mail.

At that point, I knew only two things for certain-that I could not give the letter to my aunt in its current condition, with a torn side and sweaty thumbprints, and that she could never know I had laid eyes on it.

AUNT DELIA MADE a pot roast for dinner. She refused to recognize my vegetarianism. I had tried to convince her that this wasn't a phase, and I was committed to making my life permanently meatless. I pushed the green beans to the edge of my plate, forming a straight green line, then smashed my mashed potatoes with the back of my fork as the white starch oozed between the metal tines.

"Do not play with your food, Gwyn." Aunt Delia picked up her glass of iced tea and tilted her head to peer at me over the rim of her glasses.

"Ah, sorry," I said, caught off-guard. I stabbed a green bean with my fork and brought it to my mouth.

"Trisha, how are things at the hospital?" Uncle Beckett asked my mom, seeming to break the silence with harmless conversation.

"Going well." She split a roll with her fingers and smeared butter inside. "We finally hired three new nurses this week and another day receptionist."

"That's good to hear. And Gwyn, how was the florist?" Uncle Beckett picked up a cherry tomato and popped it in his mouth.

"Um, fine. Mrs. Jenkins asked me to design—"

"I believe this is yours. It was in the mail tray," Aunt Delia interrupted.

She slid the envelope from Massachusetts College of Art and Design across the table with her fingers. "It appeared to have already been opened, so I took the liberty of investigating. You should not leave important documents lying around. There's no turning back now, I see. You'll be leaving."

I inhaled sharply. I had no idea how the letter ended up with her mail. I remembered putting the letter in my purse, at least I thought so.

Mom placed her fork on the table with an audible clang. "Delia, you opened Gwyn's mail? She's old enough to have some privacy."

Uncle Beckett ran the open palm down the length of his face, which he did when he was exasperated. He had lived with us so long, he knew the signals of an escalating argument.

"Trisha, the letter was opened. If Gwyn did not want me to read it, she should not have placed it along with my mail."

"I didn't mean to—I thought I'd put the letter in my purse." My carelessness surprised me. In my disorientation with the Andrew letter, I must have left the housing letter in with her mail.

Mom patted my hand. "Whether you did or didn't, the letter was addressed to you. Which doesn't give Delia the right to be nosey."

"She's under my roof," my aunt said firmly.

"Don't start that again, Delia," Mom replied, raising her voice. "I'm sick of you pulling that line."

"You could have chosen to leave many years ago, but you did not. You need us, admit it, Trisha."

"Delia, I'm tired of having the same argument. I stayed—we stayed—because Gwyn needed a family. You needed a family." My mom stared directly at her sister. "After everything—"

The air held weight like one of those Southern spring days when the temperature increases twenty degrees in an hour, and you're still wearing a heavy coat.

"Trish," Aunt Delia interrupted. "You couldn't have raised her on your own. You threw what Mother and Papa gave you away."

Mom stood up and pressed her hands on the table. She bit her lower lip before she released an audible exhale. "For crying out loud. Beckett, aren't you going to say something?"

"You know I care about all three of you." Uncle Beckett rose from his chair. "But this is your situation to resolve. I'm going to my study."

Uncle's door screeched to a close. Mom leaned over the table and picked up the envelope, removed its contents, and began to read. "Why, Gwyn, this is wonderful. You are in the honors dorm."

Mom smiled, handing me the letter. She squeezed my hand and turned to give my aunt a sharp glare.

"Living with a roommate should be easy for you," she added. "No roommate could be as irritating as my sister."

"Isn't it about time you leave for work, Trisha?"

Aunt Delia locked eyes with Mom. Seconds passed. My aunt crossed her arms and leaned back in the chair.

"I guess that's my cue to leave. Love you, Gwynnie." Mom kissed my forehead.

After Mom strolled out, Aunt Delia and I sat at the dinner table in silence. Her eyes were fixed on me. I turned away, and my gaze landed on the large walnut desk, which I could see clearly through the archway to her office. With the hutch included, the desk stood almost six feet tall. The hutch contained Aunt Delia's antique books. Beneath the roll-top desk were two drawers, where Aunt Delia placed her mail when she didn't know I was watching. As if light began to pour from the unopened drawers, my thoughts rallied. After the years of arguments between Mom and Delia, the root had to be more than money, otherwise we were all a petty bunch. The money, the paintings, her secret mail, Andrew, could they all be connected? The letter was addressed to Delia after all. Maybe there were more letters just waiting to be found.

My chest heaved.

"Gwyn."

"Wh-What?"

"You are staring at my secretary as if you are waiting for something to grow from the wood."

"Uh, no, ma'am. I, uh, was just thinking how beautiful it is."

"That secretary is nearly a hundred years old."

I stood and began to frantically gather the plates, knocking silverware on the floor and nearly spilling a glass of tea.

"Leave the dishes," Aunt Delia said firmly. "Go outside. You look like you need some air."

7
ANDREW

*U*nlike me, Cher slept soundly at the foot of my bed, her contented purr merging with the whirl of the ceiling fan. I laid awake, staring at the glow-in-the-dark stars, which I stuck to my bedroom ceiling when I was twelve.

My biggest concern in middle school was whether or not I would be invited to Judy Finnegan's birthday party. Today, birthday presents and popularity contests were the least of my concerns. My life was changing. Not only would I be defying my aunt to attend school in Boston, but I knew this burning mystery would consume my thoughts until I investigated further.

I stared at the glowing stars for an hour before convincing myself I should creep down the stairs and search through Aunt Delia's secretary. As a child, I hardly noticed the roll-top desk, and now I constructed a mental map of each drawer.

Being careful not to wake Cher, I rooted through my closet to find a flashlight. I slowly descended the stairs hoping not to startle the creaky floorboards. A furry body brushed against my lower leg, and I grabbed the handrail to keep my balance. Cher stopped and turned toward me. Her eyes glowed in the darkness. Then she darted off, disappearing into the night. Once I reached the bottom, I directed the flashlight's beam to the baseboard of the foyer and rounded the corner to the dining room.

I wedged the flashlight under my arm, pulled out the secretary drawer, and placed it on the floor. The drawer was filled with mail, which Aunt Delia had organized into stacks, each one bound with a rubber band. A group of children's holiday cards caught my attention. I removed the rubber band and a sticky note with the words: "Gwyn's cards." On top was the Halloween card from summer-camp Brian. Underneath Brian's card were Valentine and Easter cards from my dad for each year of elementary and middle school. After all her negative talk about Dad, it surprised me that Aunt Delia kept the cards. I wanted to take them to my room, but if she opened the drawer and saw the cards missing, it would arouse too much suspicion, so I replaced them.

I thumbed through several large stacks of Christmas cards from random people, a bundle of old credit card bills, and a stack of five beige envelopes. The heat rose in my extremities. If someone stood next to me, I swear they could have heard my racing heart. The envelopes perfectly matched the one I had inadvertently torn earlier today. Each letter had the name "Sr. Susan" in the return address and a Philadelphia postmark.

I shivered. I could not believe how easily I located the letters, but then again, before this afternoon, I never knew there was anything to find.

The letters were in order of the most recent postmark. I opened the first letter, careful not to tear this one.

May 15, 1988

Delia,

Andrew graduated from the University of Pennsylvania the first week of May with honors. You would be proud of him.

In peace,
Sr. Susan

I read the letter, mouthing the words, giving each special emphasis. Whoever this Andrew was, Aunt Delia had been receiving reports on him for years. I could not imagine that Uncle Beckett was privy to these letters. He could not keep a secret.

My mom hid all my Christmas presents at a neighbor's house, because if Uncle Beckett saw my gifts, I would know each one well before Christmas morning. And if Uncle Beckett was proud of someone, as apparently, we were to be of this Andrew, the whole town would know it.

I removed the other four letters from their respective envelopes and tucked them in my bathrobe pocket. I sorted the empty envelopes in the order of the postmarks, wrapped them in the rubber band, and replaced the stack in its original position in the drawer. I doubted Aunt Delia reread the letters, as the stationary showed little wear. If she could see the stack of envelopes in their proper place, empty or not, I should be safe.

The house seemed different in the middle of the night, no creaking floors from humans walking about or the whir of electricity illuminating the lights. The curtains were pulled to only allow a sliver of moonlight to streak across the hardwood floor. The pewter chandelier hung motionless, The air conditioning cycled off which pronounced the silence that filled the room. I jumped when the grandfather clock chimed. It was three A.M.

After carefully closing the secretary drawer, I tiptoed to my room, with one hand clutching the pocketed letters.

I tightly held the doorknob, which prevented the door from making a loud creaking sound when it closed. Propping the flashlight on my bed, I spread the letters across the bed in order of their dates, including the one I found today. Annoyed by the light, Cher jumped off my pillow and found refuge in my closet.

The earliest letter was written in 1966 and referred to Andrew taking his first steps. The next three letters told of Andrew's first day of kindergarten and his graduations from junior high and high school. All the letters were handwritten in the same perfect script, each no more than two sentences. If the letter was important enough to send, why didn't she go into more detail?

I took the notebook from my desk and calculated years and ages. Aunt Delia turned nineteen in 1965. It did not make sense that she would have any relationship with a child named Andrew who lived in Pennsylvania. Maybe Susan and Aunt Delia were old high school friends, and Susan wanted to stay in touch—although this seemed like a strange way of doing so. Or, possibly, Andrew was Susan's secret love child, and Delia was the only person who knew the truth of his origins. Although, I couldn't imagine someone being intimate friends with Aunt Delia to the point of revealing a personal secret.

With little I could resolve tonight, I placed the letters in the front pouch of my backpack, shoved the bag under my bed, and turned off the flashlight. My head met my pillow, longing for a dreamless sleep.

"Denise, what do you make of this?"

I handed the letters to Denise, as she lounged cross-legged in my beanbag chair.

"God, this is so weird. Have you told your mom?" She brought the letters close to her face and then held them at arm's length as if an amazing revelation could pop out at any time.

"I have this gut feeling I'm supposed to find out who Andrew is. I can't explain why, and I can't tell Mom until I know the truth. It's not worth making everyone mad until I know the whole story, you know?"

"Yeah, I get it." Denise shuffled through the letters, rereading them for the fifth time. "On one hand, the letters seem insignificant—I mean they are so short and almost unemotional, yet, why would Delia never have mentioned him? Andrew must mean something to her; otherwise, she wouldn't have kept these."

"I don't know. Maybe Aunt Delia thought Andrew wasn't worth mentioning, because we probably wouldn't meet him anyway. Like a second cousin once removed or whatever. He might not even be related."

"I still think you need to get to the bottom of this. There might be something you could use here—you know, to your advantage."

"Denise, I'm not going to blackmail my aunt, despite how much she drives me crazy."

"Good God, Gwyn, I'm not talking about blackmail. She might be more likely to concede if she knows you caught her hiding something big." Denise gave me a sly smile and rubbed the edge of her hoop earring. Her green eyes, a color most people could only achieve with contacts, brightened with excitement. "Do you want to be paying loans for the rest of your life?"

I rolled my eyes. "Let's not go all Godfather here. My uncle said there was more to Aunt Delia than what she shows on the outside. What if the secret isn't about someone else but about herself?" I ran my hand through my thick hair, my fingers almost getting caught in the unruly curls.

"Really, you think your straitlaced aunt is hiding a deep, dark secret?"

"Not like a scandalous secret, but one that would bring down all of her rigidity. I really think if I could get into the trunk I told you about, I believe I can begin to piece some of this together."

"What do you think is in there?"

"I don't know. Uncle Beckett said it's her hope chest from when she grew up."

"Yeah, if Andrew is a cousin or something, you might find some family pictures." Denise paused and read the letters again. "I think I can help you create a diversion, so you have time to sneak upstairs."

"What are you thinking?"

"You know how Uncle Beckett loves Danny."

"Uh huh, who doesn't?" I gave a smug smile, and Denise playfully glared at me.

My classmates in our small town thought Danny was exotic. His family moved to Riverbend four years ago from Pasadena, California. Every girl wanted Danny from the day he set foot on the Riverbend High School campus, and Denise got him.

Blond, floppy-haired Danny fell in love. When they began dating two years ago, I thought Denise's relationship with her awkward best friend would be forgotten, but that didn't happen. Danny had proven to be a good friend, and he never made me feel like a third wheel.

"The three of us—you, me, and Danny—will go to the bookshop together. Danny can get Uncle Beck talking about his science fiction collection or something long enough for you to go upstairs."

"Denise, I have to be honest here. I'm okay with you telling Danny that I found something, but I'm not ready to share the content of the letters with anyone else."

"I promise, I won't. This is just between us."

"Thanks, but, um, you don't think he'll ask any questions?"

"Danny? No, he'll follow along with whatever I say. He's

wrapped around my little finger." Denise smiled and wiggled her pinky finger at me.

"That's the truth. He'll follow you anywhere." I gathered the letters and placed them in a manila envelope. "Okay, so we'll do this on Saturday."

Denise squeezed my shoulder. "Saturday, it is."

8
THE TRUNK

I had never intentionally deceived my uncle. I was so nervous that Denise decided she should drive us to the bookshop. Danny sat in the back seat and leaned forward to rest his elbows on the console between the two front seats. He and Denise were animatedly discussing an episode of MTV's *The Real World*. I cracked my knuckles as I stared out of the Volkswagen Jetta's passenger window.

Danny nudged the back of my head with his hand. "Would you snap out of it? Everything's going to be fine. What could go wrong with the two of us here?" He gestured to himself and Denise. They both attempted to hold in laughter as I shot them a harsh glare.

"Yeah, Gwyn, it will be fine. Let us do all the talking," Denise said, "As long as you can get back in twenty minutes or so, we can hold Uncle Beck."

"I'm not concerned about the plan. This is the first time that I've lied to him." I intertwined my fingers until my knuckles had turned white.

"It's not lying, really," Danny said. "You're just not telling him what you are doing. At any rate, you're not snooping through his stuff—you're snooping through your aunt's, and you've already done that."

"So, what are you saying?" I turned to look at Danny.

"Nowhere to go but down. You're already on the path to hell;

might as well finish the job. Because when Delia finds out, boy." Danny briskly rubbed his hands together.

"Danny, would you stop it? Gwyn isn't going to hell for this. Don't make her more nervous than she already is." Denise shot Danny a squinty glare in the rearview mirror. "Don't listen to him. Keep in mind, Aunt Delia's the one hiding something. You're just trying to find out the truth. Remember that gut feeling you told me about?"

"Yeah, but it still doesn't make me feel any better."

"Gwyn, look, I don't know what you found of your Aunt Delia's, and I don't want to know." Danny paused, with deep sincerity in his brown eyes. "But I do know you are a good person, and if you are trying to seek the truth, then that is what's important."

"Thanks, Danny."

"Okay, we're here." Denise shifted the Volkswagen into park. "Show time."

We saw Uncle Beckett talking to a customer through the large glass window at the storefront as we approached. The customer leaned in close, hanging on Uncle Beckett's every word. I would bet ten dollars that the customer was a tourist.

I regretted wearing jeans in the middle of June, as my perspiration from sheer nerves caused the fabric to cling to my skin. Danny opened the bookshop door, which triggered the shopkeeper's bell to jingle. Uncle Beckett's smile widened when he saw the three of us, and he left the customer to peruse the biographies alone.

"Why, isn't this a wonderful surprise?" Uncle Beckett said, welcoming us with his open arms. "Hello, Denise, and Danny. I haven't seen you since the graduation ceremony." He squeezed my shoulder. "So, to what do I owe this pleasure?"

Uncle Beckett's excitement made me feel even more terrible about my plans. My life of breaking and entering quickly escalated over the past week. I fiddled with the clasp on my bracelet to avoid making eye contact.

"How's my favorite girl?" Uncle Beckett kissed me on the top of the forehead. I didn't look up.

"Great, Uncle." I forced a smile.

"And Danny, what have you been up to?"

"I'm still a lifeguard at the country club. My job consists of mostly telling eight-year-olds not to throw food in the pool and keeping the middle-schoolers from killing each other." Danny gave an overdramatized cringe. "And hanging out with this one." Danny put his arm around Denise's waist. Denise playfully hit Danny in the stomach with her purse, and he reacted as if he had been kicked by a horse.

Uncle Beckett laughed heartily.

"Actually—" I paused and coughed, trying to give my mind time to catch up with my tongue. "Danny, um—"

"Yeah, Danny wanted a copy of Asimov's *I, Robot*," Denise said with enthusiasm. "His father's birthday is coming up, and he's a big science fiction fan."

"Yeah, big science fan." Danny gave me the side-eye.

I covered my face in embarrassment for Danny. I guess he missed the lesson in biology class that science and *science fiction* cannot be used interchangeably. I also knew Danny had never heard of Asimov, but he was about to learn more about the author than he ever wanted to know.

Uncle Beckett's eyes brightened. "I have several first editions in the science fiction section, that is, depending on how much you want to pay, my boy." Uncle Beckett put his arm around Danny's shoulder and led him across the store. "How about Heinlein or Arthur C. Clarke?"

As their backs were turned, Denise waved me away and mouthed, "Go now."

I tightly held the strap of my empty backpack that draped over my right shoulder. I moved toward the counter, unhooked the key with my free hand, and carefully ascended the staircase. Uncle Beckett's warning about the missing handrail echoed in my mind.

Muffled voices rose from the bookstacks below. I did not turn on the light above the staircase in case it alerted my uncle, so I had to rub my hand over the doorknob to find the keyhole.

The stillness of the room overwhelmed me. A breeze touched my cheek, sending a shiver down my spine. My eyes darted around the room searching for a crack in the wood to explain the breeze. This was no time to think about ghosts. I pushed aside my urge to look again at Aunt Delia's paintings lining the wall. I only had about fifteen minutes to find clues about Andrew.

I knelt in front of the trunk and popped open the center latch with a small pocketknife my dad had given me on my fifteenth birthday. Thankfully, my aunt had purchased a cheap lock. I blew the dust off the top of the trunk and lifted the lid to reveal the blue blanket and a Christmas stocking embroidered with Delia's name in beautiful script. Tucked underneath the blanket was a white Thalheimers shoebox. In middle school, Mom and Aunt Delia took me to the department store's going out of business sale in Richmond. The frenzy of women rooting through racks of clothing and jewelry was both comical and overwhelming.

Inside the box were photographs and letters. I slipped it in my backpack, knowing I did not have time to scrutinize its contents right now. I glanced down at my watch. I had already been in the room for eight minutes—seven left. My heart kept double-time with each click of the second hand.

I turned in the direction of the paintings. A blue blanket, which had an unusual pattern of orange, yellow, and brown squares, caught my eye. It reminded me of autumn leaves falling on the surface of a lake. Uncle Beckett had not shown me the paintings that were hidden underneath this covering.

Curious, I carefully removed the blanket. Each canvas underneath displayed an oil painting of the same young man. On the back of these canvases, Delia had written: *Adam, 1964*. The paintings were beautiful, with color combinations reminiscent of the French Impressionists. Two of the paintings were full-body images of Adam lounging by the river, and the other two were portraits of Adam's striking face. He had a chiseled jawline, with a dimple in the left cheek. One portrait canvas was no larger than the size of a notebook, so I slipped that in my backpack as well.

I quickly replaced the remaining paintings, blanket, and Christmas stocking and hurried to the door before securing my backpack on both shoulders. My hands, sticky with perspiration, made it challenging to turn the lock on the doorknob. I descended the stairs in almost a squat to keep from being seen while periodically peering over the handrail to determine where my uncle and friends were in the store.

Uncle Beckett stood on his toes to look over the stacks. "Did we lose Gwyn? I was so engrossed in our conversation; I did not see her slip away."

I immediately sat down on a stair and held my breath.

"She went to the restroom. She wasn't feeling well; you know, female things," Denise said nonchalantly.

"Say no more," Uncle Beckett said, clearly uncomfortable. In my experience, mentioning *female things* was a good way to get a man to stop asking questions. Thankfully, Denise did well under pressure.

At the bottom of the staircase, I crawled to the checkout counter and returned the key. I could not see Uncle Beckett, so I thought it safe to stand and proceed toward the storefront.

"Ah, there you are." Uncle Beckett smiled at me.

"Yeah, there you are." Danny glanced at me with obvious annoyance.

My uncle put his arm around my shoulder. "Are you feeling better? You look flushed, sweetheart."

"You know, Uncle, female stuff."

Uncle Beckett leaned toward Danny for sympathy. "I lived most of my adult life with three women. You'd think I'd be used to having this conversation."

"Yeah, I feel sorry for you." Danny gave him a manly pat on the shoulder.

"I think it's time we go, Uncle Beck," Denise said, hooking her arm around my elbow. "We should take Gwyn home."

"I hope you feel better." Uncle Beckett gave me a sympathetic smile.

"Love you, Uncle."

"Love you, too, Gwynnie."

Danny held the door open as Denise and I walked outside to face the June heat.

"It better have been worth it, because you owe me." Danny held up a vintage edition of *I, Robot* with a sales receipt peeking out from inside the front cover.

I cringed. "How much did it cost?"

"You don't want to know."

9
THE SHOEBOX

"Bye, Danny," I yelled through the open passenger window as we dropped Danny off at his house. "I'm sorry about the book. I'll pay you back. Promise!"

"Whatever, Gwyn," he replied, waving us away. "Just be glad I like you!"

Denise's car sputtered as she shifted into drive. I hugged my backpack to my chest. During a sleepover at Denise's house in the eighth grade, we dyed our hair blue, which happened to be the same color as my backpack. We'd been thirteen and impulsive, but at least we had the foresight not to use permanent hair color. Aunt Delia had been so furious that she did not allow me to attend school until the dye had completely faded. I washed my hair nineteen times, but I still missed two days of school and a class field trip to the planetarium.

I thought about the portrait of Adam. I could only imagine my punishment if Aunt Delia knew I had taken something from her more valuable than her niece's natural hair color.

"Thanks for not telling Danny about what I found." I rubbed the edges of the shoebox through the bag's nylon. "He was a really good sport about it all."

"You're welcome, and your uncle is a good salesman. He almost talked Danny into buying two books. I finally had to step in." Denise looked at me and waited for a response, but my mind was elsewhere. "I was starting to get worried. You were gone for a while. What did you find? Hey, earth to Gwyn."

Denise tapped me on the head. "Are you okay?"

I drew in a deep breath and released. "No, yeah, I'm fine. I don't exactly know yet. I didn't have time to really look through everything. I took a shoebox and a small portrait Aunt Delia had done. The box had a bunch of letters and pictures, and a small book."

"Well, that should give you some clues."

"I hope so," I said as I fiddled with the *I love D.C.* keychain attached to my backpack.

"Um, did you want me to be there when you go through the box?" Denise asked.

"I think I really need to do this by myself."

"Are you sure? It could be pretty intense. Who knows what you'll dig up?"

"Yes, I'll be fine."

I leaned my temple on the passenger window as we drove past our former high school. We had only graduated a few weeks ago, but the building seemed so distant to me now. The brick structure appeared to droop in the shadow of the empty student parking lot. I knew the loneliness of that building. Granted, I had friends and good grades, but I believed my worth lay in a world beyond the one I longed to escape from.

I jumped when Denise touched my forearm.

"Okay, but you know where I am if you need me."

"I know, thanks. If we need to make any more road trips, I'll be sure to call you." I turned and smiled at my friend.

"There's the Gwyn I know and love. The one that smiles."

I poked Denise and made the meanest face I could. She playfully pushed my hand away.

"Could you quit? I'm trying to drive." Denise paused and turned up the radio. "Oh my God, this is my favorite song." She waved her arms in the air while steering with her knees. The car ran over the reflectors positioned between the road's yellow lines. I gripped the handle above the passenger door and held my backpack against my chest. Uncertainty made both me and Aunt Delia tense—maybe there was a little of her in me after all.

I shuddered. I had never thought of us having anything in common before.

AFTER ARRIVING HOME, I found Mom watching television in the family room with her legs propped on the arm of the couch. I waved to her as I ran upstairs to my bedroom, with Cher close behind. My cat scurried ahead and jumped on the bed before I could close the door and sit down. She butted her head against my hip, demanding attention. I stroked her sleek body, encouraging a loud purr.

"Are you ready to see what's in this box?" I scratched Cher's chin, and she lifted her head to look at me. "I'm not so sure either, *mon cheri.*"

I took a deep breath and sighed. I placed the box on the bed and carefully lifted the lid. A white handkerchief embroidered with blue flowers and the initials "D.S." covered the box's contents. I imagined the handkerchief as Aunt Delia's *something blue* at her wedding.

Next, I removed a copy of *Anne of Green Gables* with small paper clips marking various pages. Aunt Delia had given me a copy of this book for my eleventh birthday, which now sat on my shelf between Judy Blume's *Blubber* and S.E. Hinton's *The Outsiders*. I met Anne at the time in my life when I really needed her: middle school. I did feel like I met her. Anne made me feel less alone.

Despite being separated by three generations, Anne and I shared the same experiences. We were both raised by an older couple, headed by a woman who prized decorum over all else, and lived in the shadow of a beautiful best friend. However, I was still waiting to meet my Gilbert—the one who would value being smart over being pretty.

The box also contained a picture that appeared to be Uncle Beckett's college yearbook photo. Though much younger, he carried that sweetly serious expression, which complemented the white suit jacket and black bow tie he wore. I tucked Uncle Beckett's picture under the front cover of *Anne.*

Next, I removed two envelopes, an index card, and a heart-shaped tin container. I shook the small container; it sounded empty, so I set it aside. On the front of the first envelope was written: *For Lovely Delia; From Mrs. Brenda Quigley.* There were two pictures in the envelope of my aunt on her wedding day. She looked stunning but her eyes showed visible apprehension. In one, Aunt Delia held my six-year-old mom's hand, and Mom stared up at her big sister, who wore a simple, but beautiful, satin wedding dress and a pearl choker. The dress had a boat-neck top and sleeves that barely covered her elbows. My mom wore a frilly dress with butterfly sleeves and a ring of flowers in her hair.

In the second picture, Aunt Delia had her arm draped over the shoulder of a young woman in a bridesmaid dress. On the back of the picture, someone had written *Delia and Brenda.* I never remembered Aunt Delia mentioning a friend named Brenda, but then again, my aunt rarely discussed her childhood with me. Brenda Quigley was someone I needed to find—maybe she held the answers.

I immediately recognized the words written on the index card as Aunt Delia's perfect penmanship. She had written *The Roman Catholic Diocese of Popular Hill, PA.* I deemed the index card odd but inconsequential and returned it to the box. The letter, which I saved until last to examine, seemed to hold the most promise. It was addressed to Delia Strickland, my aunt's maiden name, at her parents' address.

My hand quivered as I read the sender's name: Adam Dale. Underneath his name, Adam wrote, *Co. B, 504th MPBn, Camp Holloway.* The postmark had faded, but I could make out a portion of the word *September* and *1964.* I removed the letter from the unsealed envelope.

> Dearest Delia,
> I miss you more than I can convey in words. Though, as you know, I've never really been good with words. That was more my brother's skill. I was sent to Camp Holloway in Gia Lia Province in South Vietnam. All I can ask is that you not read the newspapers. I cannot stand the thought of you picturing me here. Instead paint me as you remember me in the sunflower field back home. That's how I remember you from the last time I saw you that June afternoon.
> With all my love,
> Adam, 1964.

Cher placed her front paws on my leg, and she nudged my hand. "Be careful, Cher." I held the letter like it was made of porcelain.

Aunt Delia had been in love. From everything I learned about Vietnam in school, I didn't want to think about what could have happened to Adam. Maybe he survived and only came home to break her heart. Somehow, that seemed less painful than the other possible alternative.

Unfortunately, the contents of the shoebox provided little information about Andrew, giving me more questions than answers. The aunt that I perceived as having such an uncomplicated personality had suddenly become the most mysterious person I knew.

"AUNT DELIA, can I ask you something?" I said as my aunt chopped celery for chicken salad. I was seven years old.

"That's fine," she said without looking up. When Aunt Delia cooked, she piled her thick chestnut brown hair into a loose bun held together by two long hairpins. Her predictability comforted me as a child.

"Do you love Uncle Beckett like my mom and dad loved each other, before—"

"Before the divorce?"

"Uh, huh."

"It's different with us, Gwyn."

"Like, different, how?" I asked.

Aunt Delia wiped her forehead with her sleeve. She glanced at me for a moment and then continued to chop the celery, returning focus to her knife.

"Choice, Gwyn. Your mom and dad had a choice."

"Aunt Delia, which is better—your way, or Mom and Dad's?"

"One day, you will decide that for yourself." Aunt Delia picked up the cutting board and scraped the celery into the bowl with the awaiting chicken. "That's enough questions. Here's the spatula. I'll let you stir."

10
BRENDA QUIGLEY

After the events of the past weekend, I arrived at work Monday morning more distracted than usual. Thankfully, Mrs. Jenkins left for an early appointment with a bride, giving me the opportunity to call Denise, who, at this point, was my only trusted confidant.

"So, Gwyn, did you find any leads?" Denise asked.

"Just a wedding picture of my aunt with her bridesmaid. The woman's name, Brenda Quigley, is written on the envelope. Do you know any Quigleys?"

I determined that Brenda Quigley may be the only person, besides Aunt Delia, who could help me unravel the mystery surrounding my aunt's earlier life. My mom would have been too young to remember. My grandparents were dead, and my uncle wouldn't like me snooping. At any rate, he would tell me that Aunt Delia liked her privacy. I had to find Brenda Quigley, but beyond finding her, I had no plan.

"God, I don't think I'd want to go through life with Quigley as my last name," Denise scoffed.

"Come on, it's not that bad. Have you heard of them?"

I could hear Denise smacking gum over the receiver. "No, sorry. Hey, aren't you at work?"

"Yeah, Mrs. Jenkins went out to an appointment."

"Doesn't she have a list of addresses? You know, of people who've had flowers delivered to them?"

"Denise, you're a genius."

"I know." I could imagine Denise's cunning smile. "Get this woman's address, make a fake order, and tell Mrs. Jenkins you'll deliver it yourself."

"I know she keeps a spreadsheet with that information." I turned on the computer monitor and waited for the blue-green glow. I searched the spreadsheet files and found one labeled "customers." After opening the file, I scrolled through names until I reached the letter *Q*. "Oh my gosh. Denise, her name is here. Brenda Quigley, 134 Quail Landing, Gregory, Virginia."

"Okay," Denise said. "That's like ten miles outside of town. Figure out what day you can get these flowers delivered, and I'll drive you there."

"This is all well and good, but these flowers have to be from someone. What am I going to say?"

"There's bound to be a Mr. Quigley, but to be on the safe side, just pretend the card fell off on your way, and then she can assume what she wants."

"Denise, this could work, right?"

"I don't see why not. So, how are you going to bring up your aunt when you meet this Mrs. Quigley?"

"Well, I'm thinking I need to figure out what sort of person she is first. You know, make the delivery and feel out the situation. If she doesn't seem too—" I paused.

"You mean if she doesn't seem too much like your aunt." Denise laughed at her own joke.

"Denise, cut it out," I said, trying to suppress my own chuckle. "As I was saying, if Mrs. Quigley seems nice, like she would be willing to talk to me, I can always make an excuse to go back some other time."

"Do you think she is still in contact with your aunt? If she tells her you came by, the gig is up."

"You know, I really don't think so. Aunt Delia has never mentioned anyone by that name. I never knew Brenda Quigley existed until I found this picture." I studied the two faces in the photograph. Brenda smiled from ear to ear. Aunt Delia, however, did not smile, as I would expect someone to on her wedding day. She didn't look sad, but instead a mix of determination and boldness, like she was trying a case before a judge, not being married by one.

"Gwyn, look, I got to get to work. You figure out from Mrs. Jenkins how to get to her house, and we'll go. Man, your life has suddenly become much more exciting than mine."

"Yeah, like that's possible, Denise. Just don't tell anybody what we're doing. I can't risk Aunt Delia finding out."

"Your secret is safe with me." Denise smacked her gum as if signifying her oath and then hung up the phone.

ACQUIRING information from Mrs. Jenkins was easier than I had expected. I told her that Mr. Quigley came in to place an order while she attended the bridal appointment. Mrs. Jenkins not only gave me directions but informed me that Mrs. Quigley taught biology at Gregory High School; her husband, Steve, was a veterinarian; and they had two children, a daughter who recently married and a son in college. I told Mrs. Jenkins that Mr. Quigley had ordered an arrangement for no particular reason except to say how much his wife meant to him. She designed a beautiful bouquet of purple hydrangeas and roses, and I paid forty-five dollars in cash. I hoped giving up several hours of pay would be worth it.

I felt a little guilty about fabricating a story, but I'd become well acquainted with the feeling of guilt in recent days. I had always prided myself on my honesty, but since uncovering that first letter, I became someone else. I had lied to everyone in my life over the past two weeks. I even have been selective of what I told Denise.

I desperately wanted to discover the truth before I left for Boston. Maybe the truth would help me understand my aunt, and possibly even reconcile with her. I pushed out of my mind the idea that the truth might make things worse. If lying now meant uncovering the truth, I would make the sacrifice.

Denise and I planned to make the trip the following afternoon;

she would remain in the car, while I made the delivery.

I HOPED my discomfort during Tuesday's lunch hour with Uncle Beckett didn't show. We ate in silence, watching the noon news on his portable television. Though we typically ate in silence, today the quiet grew more excruciating because of Uncle Beckett's ignorance of my recent behavior. He ate happily, with the occasional verbal response to the television as if he expected the newscaster to be able to hear him. I, on the other hand, counted how many times I chewed each bite.

"You look really nice today, Gwyn, even though you're still wearing those black bracelets." Uncle Beckett smiled and lifted one of my black jelly bracelets with his finger and quickly let it release.

"Thanks, Uncle." I wanted to look presentable when I met Mrs. Quigley, so I toned down my usual attire. I wore a denim skirt that fell just above my knee, and a green mock-neck shirt with cap sleeves that I found in my mom's closet. I even toned down my usual bold eyeshadow. "Um, I won't need you to take me home today. Denise is picking me up from work."

"So that's why you didn't take your own car this morning." Uncle Beckett wiped his mouth with a napkin. "What are you girls up to?"

"Denise has to run an errand over in Gregory, and she wants me to ride with her."

"Are you going to that new Wal-Mart over there?" Uncle Beckett's eyes lit up.

"I could if you want me to."

"If you are, they carry these cookies I like. Here, I'll write the brand down, but don't tell your Aunt Delia; she doesn't like me eating sweets."

"I think I can handle it." I gave him a sheepish smile. At least I knew that Uncle Beckett would keep my trip to Gregory a secret since cookies were involved.

Denise picked me up promptly at three P.M. Mrs. Jenkins said I deserved to leave early because of the impressive newspaper advertisement I created. The advertisement ran in this week's paper, which apparently brought in six new customers. For a town this small, that was an achievement.

"Are you ready?" Denise asked as she bounded through the florist door.

"Yep. Ready as I'll ever be."

Mrs. Jenkins stepped out from the back room carrying Mrs. Quigley's bouquet. She sat the vase on the counter. "Okay, Gwyn, here are the instructions on how to preserve the flower's freshness, and a couple packets of plant food. Make sure you give this to her," Mrs. Jenkins said earnestly.

I nodded, taking the items from her hand.

"And Denise," Mrs. Jenkins said in a firm voice. "Drive safely— that's my reputation in your hands." She pointed to the arrangement.

"No problem, Mrs. Jenkins. Come on Gwyn, let's go."

"Bye, girls." Mrs. Jenkins waved. Denise held the door open for me as I balanced the unwieldy bouquet.

"So are you nervous?" Denise asked as she eased out of her parking space.

"What do you think?" My tone was much harsher than I intended.

"Sorry I asked." Denise's eyebrows shot up and her eyes widened in the way that indicated her irritation. "Let's talk about something else."

"Okay, sure." I paused to think of another topic of conversation. Since finding Susan's letter, I had not thought of much else. "After the delivery, we need to stop by the new Wal-Mart."

"What? I thought you had some moral opposition to mega-stores like that."

I rolled my eyes. "I still do, but finding answers takes priority right now. I said you had to run errands as my excuse for going to Gregory, and Uncle Beckett asked if I could pick up his favorite cookies at Wal-Mart. You would have thought I handed him a hundred dollars instead of promising to bring back a four dollar pack of cookies. I couldn't say no."

"And I suppose he also asked you to sneak in the sweets, so

Aunt Delia won't see."

"Yeah, how did you know?"

"Lucky guess. What's one more thing to hide from her?" Denise gave me a smirk, and I let out a little chuckle.

I remained quiet on the drive to the Quigley's, except to interrupt Denise's story to read the directions. She was going on about some neighbor's chickens getting loose and how she had ruined her manicure, or was it her shoes? I couldn't repeat the story if I tried, as I was so preoccupied with my half-baked plan to talk to Brenda Quigley.

"Okay, here it is. That driveway on the left, next to that red mailbox." I pointed with enthusiasm. The driveway curved toward the left side of the house, ending at a two-car garage. Denise parked the car so she could see the Quigley's front door just in case she needed to intervene on my behalf.

"Stay in the car, Denise. I won't be too long."

"You can do this. You look good by the way," Denise said.

"Thanks, Denise. I appreciate that."

The Quigley's lived in a white brick ranch house, which sat on several acres that included a modest-sized barn and a fenced, horse pasture. Camellia bushes, with bright magenta blooms, were positioned on each side of the front stairs. Affixed to the front windows were black iron flower boxes that matched the handrail leading to the front door. I awkwardly held the vase in the crook of my arm and rang the doorbell. I leaned back and glanced at Denise sitting in the car; she waved reassuringly.

The front door opened, not by a middle-aged woman, but a young man. He stood barefoot and wore faded blue jeans and a white T-shirt. The whiteness of his shirt made his grayish blue eyes even more remarkable. He was beautiful. I stared at him, gape-mouthed. The young man ran his hand through his thick auburn hair and yawned.

"Um, hey," I said.

"Hey, yourself. I assume you're here to make a delivery." He gestured to the bouquet.

"Oh, yeah." I suddenly became aware of the vase's heaviness. "I have a delivery for Brenda Quigley from The Fragrant Garden, the florist in Riverbend."

"Brenda's my mom." Without taking his hand off the door, the young man turned and yelled, "Mom!"

"I'm coming, Isaac. I've told you before not to yell through the house when we have guests." Mrs. Quigley approached the door and instinctually held out her hand to shake mine, but my hands were too full to greet her with a handshake. She patted my shoulder instead.

"I see you met my rude son," Mrs. Quigley added with a smile.

"Yes, ma'am," I replied.

"This is Isaac, our youngest, and our little surprise." Mrs. Quigley pinched Isaac's cheek.

"Mom," Isaac said, sounding annoyed. "Do you have to tell everyone that?"

"I have to explain this gray hair somehow. Now, let me take these beautiful flowers from you, dear."

I recognized Mrs. Quigley from the photograph. Despite being over thirty years older, she still had the same bright smile. Mrs. Quigley was dressed more as a potter than a high school biology teacher. She wore straight knee-length khaki shorts and a green bohemian tunic with embroidered flowers around the neckline. A lengthy string of dark brown seed beads hung around her neck. Her long, gray hair, tied at the base of her neck, complemented her smooth ivory skin.

"Yes, truly beautiful. It looks like the work of Mrs. Jenkins. Am I right? I always use her, even if she is in another town." Mrs. Quigley rotated the vase in her hands, admiring the flowers from all sides.

"Yes, ma'am," I said. "She's the best."

Isaac's eyes were locked on me, as if he was trying to read my thoughts. His gaze unnerved me.

"Yes, she is. Now, who are these from?" Mrs. Quigley turned the vase in her hands searching for a card.

"Let me check," I said. I ran my thumb over the empty plastic card holder in the vase and patted down my pockets.

"I'm sorry, Mrs. Quigley, the card is missing," I said, faking panic, as I foresaw my perfect plan about to be ruined. "But uh, here are the plant food packets."

Isaac maintained eye contact with me. "They're from me, Mom.

I knew how hard you worked on Veronica's wedding reception, and I thought you deserved them."

Isaac winked, letting me know that he saved me. My heart began to race, and heat flooded my body. I didn't know whether my body was reacting to his arrogance or my sudden attraction to him. My high school biology teacher said attraction boiled down to a chemical reaction in the brain, which was as unpredictable as it was inconvenient.

"Well, aren't you the sweetest?" Mrs. Quigley beamed at her son. "Let me put these on the dining room table. Now, don't go anywhere, young lady; I didn't get your name."

Isaac and I stood in silence. He still held the door open with his hand, and I could feel him watching me. I fixed my gaze on the throw rug in the foyer to avoid making eye contact. Images of blue birds edged the circular rug, their beaks open as if about to break out in song. I swear the rug birds were laughing at our awkwardness. Isaac slapped a mosquito that landed on his forearm.

"That was louder than expected," he mumbled.

"Yeah, it happens," I said, as if standing uncomfortably in the doorway with someone you just met while slapping mosquitoes was normal.

"Okay, I'm back," Ms. Quigley said. "Now, what is your name, dear?"

"Oh, my name's Gwyn."

"Well, nice to meet you, sweetheart." Mrs. Quigley nudged her son with her elbow.

"Isn't that right, Isaac?"

"Oh, yeah, nice to meet you." Isaac gave a slight smile.

"Okay, bye." I waved and hurried to Denise's awaiting car. I slipped into the passenger seat as quickly as I could.

"Okay, so how did it go?" Denise asked eagerly. "Is she nice?"

"Fine. Mrs. Quigley was very nice, but her son, well, he's a little odd. He kept staring at me; it was so awkward."

"Yeah, I noticed. But you have to admit, he is hot."

"Well, maybe a little." I smiled and turned to look at the Quigley's closed front door.

As if shaking myself out of a daydream, I said, "Come on, Denise, we have to go to Wal-Mart."

11
BAGELS

Despite the compliments I received from wearing my mom's outfit the day before, I defaulted to my eclectic wardrobe. I never felt comfortable wearing figure-hugging feminine clothes. I chose a pair of denim shorts rolled at the knee, a white cotton button-down shirt and a men's suit vest I bought at a thrift store. I removed Aunt Delia's shoebox from my backpack and hid it in my closet under a pile of sweaters. I left the letters from Susan in the front pocket of my backpack as a constant reminder of my summer mission. Lastly, I slid my sketch pad and a box of colored pencils in the largest pouch.

I found my place at the breakfast table beside my mom and across from Aunt Delia. Uncle Beckett's bowl sat on his placemat with a few remaining bits of oatmeal stuck to the inside.

"Where's Uncle Beckett?" I asked.

"He's being interviewed by a reporter from *The Riverbend Tribune*." Aunt Delia stirred creamer into her coffee, then tapped the rim of the mug with the spoon to remove any potential drips.

"Oh that'll be fun for him." I turned to look at Mom. She yawned and rubbed her eyes. "Boy, you look beat."

"The storms last night caused major problems and a lot of bad car accidents. The waiting room was packed for hours."

"You need to get some rest, Trisha." Aunt Delia's tone teetered between motherly and patronizing.

"I'm going to, Delia. I wanted to see my daughter before she left for work. We've hardly seen each other since the summer began."

I stirred cinnamon into my oatmeal. "It's okay, Mom. I understand. Hey, did you see my ad in the paper—the one I made for Mrs. Jenkins?"

"I did, actually. Your Aunt Delia cut it out and hung it on the refrigerator. See." Mom turned to point to the quarter-page newspaper advertisement, which covered the majority of Aunt Delia's church announcement flier.

"You hung my ad, Aunt Delia? I didn't know that."

"What, that I took interest in my niece's accomplishments?" Aunt Delia asked, giving me a wry smile before bringing her coffee mug to her lips

"Well, I mean, you never really—"

Mom touched my hand, indicating that I should stop talking. "I'm glad I got to see you this morning. I'm going upstairs to get some sleep." She yawned again as she rose from the table. "Oh, Gwyn, I almost forgot. Uncle Beckett told me to tell you, 'Thanks.' Do you know what that's about?"

"Yeah, I did a favor for him yesterday." Uncle Beckett had secrets, too, but they were mostly about desserts.

"Gwyn, you spoil that man too much." Aunt Delia straightened the collar of her blue silk blouse.

"Who—Uncle Beckett?" I asked, already knowing the answer.

"I hope you are not sneaking in sweets," Aunt Delia said. "You know how I feel about that. The doctor warned him on the last visit to watch his diet."

"Yes, ma'am." I did not want to engage in an argument before nine A.M. I gathered my bowl and spoon from the table and placed them in the dishwasher. "Hey, Mom, you're off tonight, right?"

"Yes, baby, it's Wednesday. I'll see you when you get home." Mom squeezed my shoulders. "Cool eyeshadow."

"Thanks. The color's called gunmetal."

Aunt Delia leaned back and crossed her arms. "That's quite a name."

"Aunt Delia, I'm leaving for work." I stood and pushed my chair under the table. "Um, I hope you have a nice day." With my hand on the doorknob, I turned to look at her and waited for a response. I thought her silk top would be much more flattering if it were not buttoned to her neck. But then again, that's one thing Aunt Delia and I had in common—neither of us wanted to be perceived as too girly. "Okay, then, I need to go."

"Wait, Gwyn," she said, turning in her chair toward me. "I don't want you to think I do not care about your achievements."

"I know, Aunt Delia."

"No, I don't think you do. I want you to understand. I believe that when raising a child, one shouldn't puff up her ego, overly spoil the child. That would give the child a false impression of what the world is truly like."

I closed my eyes, squeezed the bridge of my nose, and released it. "Aunt Delia, is this about the advertisement, or something else—like me moving away?"

"I don't want you to be disappointed. You can be extremely talented but the outcome still might fall short of your expectations." Delia stood and straightened her summer-weight tweed skirt. "It's better to be realistic when making decisions."

"Well, if I am disappointed, at least I know I tried. That's all I can ask of myself." I opened the screen door and stepped on the landing. "I'll see you tonight, Aunt Delia."

FOR A WEDNESDAY MORNING, the florist shop was busy. We had a total of five walk-ins and ten phone orders. One might think a town with a population of less than 5,000 couldn't support a row of small businesses but somehow, Riverbend managed to do it. Between recording orders, I sketched the storefront window and door from where I sat behind the counter. I drew each backwards green letter affixed to the glass door, as well as the large birdcage-shaped topiary filling the window space. The late morning sunlight illuminated a triangular wedge on the floor.

After a few moments, the wedge awkwardly changed form. I raised my head to find Isaac Quigley staring at me through the window. He held up a paper bag with the logo of the local bagel shop.

I squinted and tilted my head, my face expressing obvious surprise. Isaac imitated me, and I couldn't help but smile.

I strolled to the store entrance. Not wanting to appear too eager, I opened the door just enough to stand in the space between the door and its frame. I crossed my arms and locked eyes with my visitor.

"You seem like a girl who enjoys a good bagel," Isaac said. I wondered how long it took him to come up with that pick-up line.

"Well, aren't you a little presumptuous?"

"I don't think so." Isaac smiled. His eyes wandered from my gunmetal eyeshadow to my black low-top Converse sneakers, adorned with beaded safety pins. "It looks like your style has changed since yesterday."

"What is that supposed to mean?" I asked, crossing my arms.

"Nothing, it's fine. You look great, just different than when I — "

"You better stop there." Without thinking, I placed the palm of my hand on his chest. We both jumped back slightly, surprised by the contact. "Um, maybe your mom was right," I said in a low voice.

"About what?"

"That you're a bit rude." I looked up at him and smiled. "My boss is in the back working on an order, but you can come in."

"Okay, sounds good." Isaac reached above my head and pushed the door open. The knuckles of his other hand grazed my back, triggering a shiver.

"So, this is where you work?" he asked, placing the bag of bagels on the counter.

"Yes, five days a week in the summer and afternoons over the school year."

I hurried to close my sketch pad and gather my colored pencils, but he lightly tapped my wrist to stop me.

"Let me see, please."

"Okay, but I am not promising great things." I hesitated. I wasn't ready for stuff between us to get this familiar. If a person opens an artist's sketchbook, they might as well be peering into her soul.

"No disclaimers, Gwyn."

It sounded strange for this person I hardly knew to say my name in such a comfortable way. I turned the sketch pad toward him and stepped back so he had room to turn the pages.

"I like them." Isaac stopped at a picture of a bluebird huddled under branches of a holly tree. I had drawn it from a photograph taken by Uncle Beckett, who liked to whittle wooden birds. He gave me a bluebird that sat on my desk.

"Like," I repeated. "Isn't that a word people use when they don't want to hurt someone's feelings?"

"No, I promise. I really do like your sketches. In each picture, it looks as if it's raining."

"I like how the rain makes color seem more vibrant." I held up a bluish-gray pencil, aptly named, *summer's mist*, a few inches from Isaac's face. "This one matches your eyes."

I paused, realizing I said my thoughts aloud, and quickly changed course. "I meant to say, if it were raining, this is one I would use."

I smiled and so did he.

"So, tell me, Isaac, what is the real reason you drove out here?"

"To find out, Gwyn." Isaac placed extra emphasis on my name. "What was the real reason you came to my house yesterday?"

I replaced the pencil in the box and began arranging the colors according to their position in the rainbow. Without removing my eyes from the counter, I asked, "What makes you think I had an ulterior motive other than delivering flowers?"

Isaac sauntered around the counter and stood in front of me. He leaned forward and placed his forearms on the surface. "Because if my dad or sister had sent them, they would have totally claimed it." He picked up a quarter lying on the counter and spun it.

The coin's spinning circles grew wider until it flattened.

Isaac continued in a low voice. "If it was from my aunt in Tennessee, she would have called to see if Mom received them. Process of elimination." His serious expression broke into a small smile.

"How do you know they are not from a secret admirer?" I asked.

"Come on, Gwyn, my mom is almost fifty-four."

"Your mom is attractive; that sounds like age discrimination." My attempt at a joke fell flat.

"Tell me the truth."

"Okay, but first, did you tell your mom the truth, that you lied about the flowers being from you?"

"No, I thought it was best if she just assumed I sent them. I didn't want to freak her out with any secret admirer business, and I might have needed to do a good deed after I scratched the car." He pressed down on the quarter with his index finger and moved it in circles.

"Okay, so we're both benefiting from this situation."

"The truth, Gwyn; out with it."

"How do I know if I can trust you?"

He placed his hand on my arm. "Try me."

I took a deep breath and looked up. I had always loved the stamped tin ceilings of the old downtown buildings; the florist shop was painted a pale yellow. My uncle's shop had the same ceiling, except his was brick red. I dropped my chin and met Isaac's blue eyes.

"Okay, my aunt and I are not on the best of terms right now. See, my mom and I live with her and my uncle. Ever since I was a little girl, she told me that I would always have money to go to college. Well, I got into a school in Boston, and she doesn't want me to go. So, like two months ago, to keep me from going, she told me she would only pay for college in Virginia." I stopped. I even annoyed myself when I rambled.

"Go on, your aunt does not want you to go to school in Boston; I'm listening."

I couldn't believe that I was telling a complete stranger this story —and a bit irritated that he egged me on to do just that. But he was listening, and besides Denise, no one knew the entirety of my story.

I debated on how much to tell him. The incriminating evidence I could reveal seemed to increase on a daily basis.

"Even though I've lived with my aunt most of my life, I really know nothing about her— nothing personal anyway. Like about her childhood, her adolescence. And then I accidentally stumbled upon a wedding picture of my aunt and your mom. Your mom was a bridesmaid in my aunt's wedding. Aunt Delia never spoke of her wedding or really anything prior to my mom and I moving in, and she never spoke of your mother. I thought I could learn more about my aunt if I got to know your mom, so my friend Denise helped me come up with a plan to meet her. God, I know this all sounds ridiculous. You must think I'm a mental case."

"No, I don't think you are a mental case." Isaac placed his hands over my clenched fist that rested on the counter. "Why can't you ask your aunt about my mother?"

"You don't know my Aunt Delia. First of all, she would kill me if she knew I found the picture, because that would mean I had been snooping, and second, she hates being asked about her personal life. She would call that prying."

"Alright, I think I pretty much understand, but how would knowing more about my mom help your situation?"

"Well, to be honest, at first, I snooped because I was angry. She's just made things so much harder for me. I guess I wanted to find a secret I could use as leverage." I laughed and shook my head, embarrassed that I shared such a detail. "Anger can really mess you up. But now I am honestly really intrigued. Aunt Delia has become much more interesting now that there's some mystery."

"Okay, I think I can help you, as long as I don't get stuck in the middle of a blackmail ring."

"You would help me?"

"Yeah, but no blackmail." He smiled and waved his pointer finger at me.

"Promise."

"Look, our family has a Fourth of July party every year. We cook out and then watch the fireworks over the river. There is a perfect view from our pasture."

"With your family; are you sure? I would feel a little weird. I barely know you."

"Okay, how about this. I'm a sophomore at George Mason, majoring in biology. I like cats. I despise asparagus, and as much as I hate to say this, I'm super messy, but I'm working on it." Isaac shrugged and gave me the most pitiful puppy-dog eyes, which probably have gotten him out of trouble a few times.

"I guess I could go," I said.

"You can even bring your friend Denise, if that would make you feel more comfortable." Isaac rolled my violet-colored pencil with his fingers. "It would be the perfect opportunity to get to know my mom. She really is a great person, and I'm not just saying that because I'm her son. Although, I do have great taste in flowers. Don't you agree?"

"Stop that." I laughed and lightly pushed his shoulder. "I really appreciate that you want to help me, but what's the catch? What's in it for you?"

Isaac blushed. "Well, my mom has been begging me to bring a girl over. I've never been much for dating. And then, well, you show up."

"Ah, the mutually beneficial situation." I smiled.

"Well, it works out on both ends. My mom stops nagging me and, well, you get information." We locked eyes, and I didn't blink for what seemed like several seconds.

"What if you find out you actually like me?" I asked before opening the bag of bagels and releasing the aroma of fresh bread.

"Then that would be an excellent perk." Isaac smiled widely, and for a moment, we stared at each other, allowing his words to dance in the trail of sunlight that issued through the window.

12
FIREWORKS

After coming home from work, I breathed a sigh of relief to only see my mom's Corvette in the driveway. Telling Aunt Delia about Isaac was out of the question, but I couldn't just sneak off to a Fourth of July party without someone knowing my whereabouts. Mom would allow me to go, probably even be thrilled.

I knew she never understood how her daughter grew up to be so different from her. My mom did not share my love for art and literature, although she tried to engage by asking questions about my classes. Boys had never been attracted to me like Mom experienced in high school. My clothes did not fit perfectly on my lanky, curveless body. Mom was beautiful, the perfect height, not too tall or too short. Her blond hair fell in light bouncy waves. And beyond her beauty, I knew my mom was strong. She had endured a divorce and moved here—all for my sake.

Yet, despite my mom's strength, she could not stand up to her sister. Over my first-grade Christmas break, I had gotten in trouble when an older kid in the neighborhood talked me into stealing a plastic reindeer from Mr. Granger's front yard. Mr. Granger caught me before I could even escape his driveway. As I wrote the apology letter Aunt Delia ordered, I overheard her say that Mom couldn't handle a precocious child, and my mom must have believed this about herself. After that Christmas, when it came to discipline, Mom left things to my aunt.

"Mom!" I yelled as I closed the house's side door behind me. "Mom, where are you?"

"I'm in my bedroom, folding laundry," she shouted. "Come up!"

Aunt Delia considered it barbaric to yell across the house, so when she was not at home, Mom and I yelled as much as possible. I bounded up to Mom's door.

She stood in front of a round laundry basket that rested on her bed. Anyone who saw the stack of folded shirts would immediately recognize her affinity for candy hues.

"Hey, baby. Come in and sit down."

"Mom, I need to talk to you about something." I tucked my hair behind my ear. "It's not bad or anything." I sat down in her armchair, which was upholstered with a blue-and-yellow paisley print.

"If it's not bad, don't look so serious," she teased, tossing a sock at me. I batted it away with my hand and smiled.

"It's about a guy," I said sheepishly.

Her eyes brightened. I had rarely shown interest in boys in the past, despite my mom's affinity for dating. She threw the shirt she had begun to fold into the basket. "That can wait. So, Gwyn, spill it." Mom sat down on the edge of the bed.

"Whoa, it's not like I'm announcing an engagement. Don't get so excited." I fiddled with a button on my vest. "Well, um, yesterday, I made a delivery for Mrs. Jenkins."

I needed to provide just enough information to leave my mother satisfied. If my story supplied enough detail, she would not pummel me with questions. I wanted to avoid revealing Isaac's last name in case the information got back to my aunt.

"Go on," my mom said, bright with anticipation.

"Anyway, the flowers were for a woman whose family are regular customers of Mrs. Jenkins. This lady's son answered the door. His name is Isaac." I shifted side to side, feeling too embarrassed to maintain eye contact with her. "I didn't think much of it. I was only at their house for maybe five minutes, and, well, this morning, he showed up at the florist with a bag of bagels."

"Who? Isaac?"

"Yes, Mom, Isaac. Who else would I be talking about?" I rolled my eyes.

"Gwyn, this is so cute!" She patted her knees with both palms. "Sorry, go ahead."

"He thanked me for delivering the flowers and told me his mom loved them. Apparently, the flowers were from him." I hesitated, hoping she would not hear my voice crack.

"Oh, a boy that loves his mama. You can't go wrong with that."

"For crying out loud, Mom, can you just listen?"

"Yes, honey, I won't say another word." Mom rested her forearms on her knees and leaned forward.

"We got to talking. He finished his sophomore year at George Mason. He's a biology major. Anyway, he invited me to his house for his family's Fourth of July party." Without lifting my head, I glanced up at my mom. "I, um, I told him I would go."

Excitement was written all over Mom's face. She held her breath to prevent herself from talking.

"Mom, you can say something now."

"This is so exciting! But first, I have to ask a couple parental questions." At the word *parental*, Mom mimed quotation marks with her index and middle fingers.

"Okay."

"How are you going to get there?"

"I am going to drive myself."

"Good, you know I like that. If you feel uncomfortable you can drive yourself home. How long do you think you'll stay?"

"Well, he invited me for dinner at six, but we are going to watch the fireworks, so most likely I won't be back until eleven."

"If you are going to be driving that late by yourself, it would be nice to have someone with you. I'm sure Denise and Danny would go."

"Got that one covered. Denise is coming with me."

"That sounds fine then. And don't worry; I'll keep this to myself." She squeezed next to me in the armchair and put her arms around my shoulders. "Aunt Delia doesn't need to know about this one. Okay, now we need to figure out what you are going to wear."

"I think I can do that myself, Mom."

"Huh." Her eyes moved from my vest to my shoes. "You need to at least have something on from the women's department."

I elbowed her. "My shorts most certainly are women's."

"Look, I know you wore my green shirt yesterday." She squinted, struck by an idea. "Interesting, that's what you were wearing when he met you. So, see, my clothes do work."

"Yeah, Mom, but I wore this when he asked me out." I gestured to my outfit.

"That's nice," she said, distracted. "Let's see what I have." She went to her closet and quickly sifted through the rack of clothes. "How about this?" She held up a bright pink Polo dress.

"Mom, what are you thinking? You know that's not me. It's too preppy and way too pink."

"Whatever, Gwyn. How about this?" She held up an electric blue cotton and spandex tank top with a revealing scalloped neckline. The top would barely cover my navel.

"Oh my God, Mom, no!"

Mom laughed. "Well, I'll keep this for when Charlie and I are speaking to each other again."

I covered my eyes. "That's disgusting. Put that away!"

Charlie was Mom's on-again, off-again boyfriend of five years. At the moment, he was *off*. He was four years younger and a paramedic at the hospital. I liked Charlie and honestly, I felt bad for him. My mother tended to initiate numerous break-ups.

"How about— Hey, I think this would work. You look great in this color. It complements your beautiful skin." Mom handed me a coat hanger, which held a deep purple V-neck top that appeared to be new.

I smiled at her. "Yeah, I think that one will do."

"Okay, so what will you wear with it?"

"Probably my denim skirt. The one with the frayed hem."

"Isn't that a little short?"

"Like you're one to talk." I held up the electric blue tank with two fingers at arm's length and waved it in her face. She snatched the shirt away from me, trying to contain her laughter. "The skirt comes mid-thigh, and besides I plan to wear it with my leggings."

"No, Gwyn. You know I hate those, and it's July. You'll roast."

"I need to have a little bit of me in this outfit. There's even purple in the leggings that will match the top."

The sheer leggings in question were decorated with pastel portraits of James Dean and Marilyn Monroe in the style of Andy

Warhol. Denise had bought them for me when her family visited Los Angeles last summer.

I jumped up from the armchair, ran across the hall to my room, and yelled, "It's Fourth of July, and nothing says America like Hollywood!"

Mom followed and playfully tackled me on the bed. I knew I would eventually get my way, but I wanted to let her feel she had a fighting chance.

BY FRIDAY AFTERNOON, my nervousness about attending the Quigley family party made my compulsive tendencies even more pronounced. I organized Mrs. Jenkins spools of ribbon into color, width, and the length left on the roll. I removed every dead leaf on the ivy topiary in the shop window. I found thirteen pencils in the supply drawer and sharpened them to exactly the same length. That thirteenth pencil irritated me, but it seemed wasteful to throw it away. When my mind swirled with thoughts, organizing helped me calm down.

July fourth fell on a Saturday that year, so my mom would be working. Although I hadn't mustered the courage to call Isaac to confirm our plans, I had arranged for Denise to come to my house so we could ride over together. Aunt Delia would ask more questions if I left alone. By the end of the workday, I was so jumpy that I tried to come up with a reason to skip dinner and spend the evening in my room. Walking pneumonia sounded too serious, but it would buy me a weekend alone.

"Gwyn, you've earned your pay today," Mrs. Jenkins said as she stepped out from the back room. "I've never seen the supplies more organized."

"Yeah, I don't know what came over me." I lied. Isaac came over me.

"Is your car out back?"

I nodded and picked up my backpack from underneath the counter.

"I parked on the street when I came back from the church. Tomorrow's the Brigg wedding, you know. I couldn't believe it; she has eleven bridesmaids—too many women in one place, if you ask me." Mrs. Jenkins rummaged through her purse for her car keys. "So, Gwyn, if you lock the back door, I'll take care of the front. See you next week."

"No problem." I waved as she closed the door behind her.

After leaving work, I had planned to spend a couple hours at the library looking through my college catalog before my family expected me home for dinner. Before exiting the back door, I stopped to move a spool of light green ribbon that had been placed next to a lemon yellow. I made a mental note to speak to Mrs. Jenkins on Monday about my organization plan.

I pulled the back door closed, twisted the lock, and proceeded to the car. The palm-tree-shaped I Love Orlando keychain made it easy to feel for in a dark pocket. "Got you," I said like the keys were a dog I had been chasing around. My backpack, which dangled from one shoulder, began to slip down my elbow, causing the keys to slip from my hand.

"Crap." I bent down to pick them up.

"It's about time you left. I've been waiting here thirty minutes." The familiar voice startled me. I rose too quickly and hit my head on the side-view mirror. I shut my eyes tight and opened them wide. I rubbed the top of my head, thankful that I didn't feel any sticky substance. The last thing I needed would be trying to explain to Aunt Delia why I had to get stitches in the top of my head.

"Oh God, I didn't mean to scare you!" Isaac said with obvious panic in his voice. "Are you okay?"

With my back against the car door, I sat on the gravel parking lot and pressed the palm of my hand to my throbbing head. I glanced up to see Isaac diving toward me.

He removed my hand and pushed my hair back. "Let me see."

"I'm okay, I promise." I waved him off. "I just need to sit here a minute."

"That did not go as planned. I wanted you to be happy to see me, not writhing in pain."

"If you were trying to make a good impression, you didn't quite make it." I smiled at him.

Isaac's face was flushed with embarrassment.

"It's okay." I shoved his knee. "I forgive you."

He grinned with his lips pressed together, before breaking into a wide smile.

"You showing up to my job is getting to be a habit," I said. "What's the story this time?"

Isaac sat down next to me. "I just thought that—" He picked up a stick and drew circles in the dirt parking lot, his eyes focused on the ground. "That since you are coming to my family's party, that we needed to know each other better first. You are still coming, right?" Isaac plucked a small rock, which made a light *tink* when it landed.

"Yes, I am, but remember I have investigative work to do that night, and you're under no obligation to like me," I said, trying to make a joke.

"Good." He shook his head. "Um, no, I mean not good, there's no obligation, but good you are still coming. Sorry, I'm not used to this."

"Used to what?"

"Talking to girls. I'm not really good at it."

"You're doing fine. Well, except for giving me a head injury." I smiled. "If it's any consolation, I'm not used to this either. Any male friend I have is due to the fact he is dating one of my female friends."

"Yes, that makes me feel better." Isaac turned toward me.

"I told my mom about you," I said. "Well, mainly, your first name and where you go to college. She said I could come to your party if I brought Denise with me—well, actually Denise and her boyfriend. They tend to come as a package deal."

"Does she think I'm that dangerous that you need two bodyguards?"

"No, she's just being a mom." I laughed at the thought of Mom trying to be protective; usually that job was left to Aunt Delia. "Is it okay if I bring them?"

"I'm sure that won't be a problem, as long as you're not bringing a backup date."

"Very funny. They are also my cover to get out of the house without my aunt getting suspicious." I stood up, carefully avoiding the side mirror and unlocked the door. Isaac stood as well.

"It's fine. There'll be like thirty of my family members there, and that's only counting the adults. I'll need a diversion."

"You're exaggerating, right? Thirty?"

"Um, actually, no. It's no wonder my sister and Chris eloped to Aruba."

"You're kidding."

"Well, it's what they wanted." Isaac walked to his car and sat on the hood. I followed and sat next to him with a comfortable space between us. "I went with my parents. Chris's parents were there, and another couple my sister met in law school."

"Was this recently?"

"Yeah, they got married in May. We're having a big reception for them in a few weeks."

"Eloping sounds like a great idea to me. Except mine would be a complete secret. Just me, the guy, and possibly an Elvis impersonator."

"I'm starting to like you even more." He put his arm around my shoulder, squeezed, and quickly released. The physical space between us had diminished. I needed to change the subject.

"How old is your sister?"

"Veronica just turned twenty-nine."

"Oh yeah, that's right, *you* were 'the little surprise.'"

"Shut up, I can't believe you remembered that."

"Okay, so did you have a plan for this afternoon, or is this it—sitting on the hood of your car?"

"Uh, no, I almost forgot. Get up." I stood and followed Isaac to his trunk. He opened it and held up two fishing poles in one hand and a closed bucket of bait in the other.

"You've got to be kidding me—fishing?"

"Yeah, what are you, one of those girls who is afraid of a little dirt?"

"Heck, no. I can bait a hook. That's my grandpa's lasting legacy. He took me fishing almost every weekend before he died."

"Okay then, girlie, you're on." He slammed down the trunk door.

"Get in your car; I'll follow you to the pier." I tossed my backpack in the passenger seat and peeled out of the dirt parking lot after him.

The public pier was accessible along the river on the east side of town. On Saturday mornings, fathers lined the pier, teaching their young sons how to bait a hook and the art of patience. However, on a humid mid-summer afternoon, rarely did anyone set foot on the wood planks. Isaac and I sat on the far end of the pier, which was lined on two sides by tall marsh grass. Dragonflies landed on the water's surface only to rise a second later.

"Hey, Isaac, can I ask you something?"

He handed me an orange soda from the cooler. "Sure."

"Did your parents pressure you? I mean, about attending a certain college?"

"Not really. I know my dad would have loved for me to go to the same college he and mom did, but he never said as much." Isaac paused to untwist the cap from his soda. "Actually, my parents were the types that didn't give us much direction on those issues. They wanted us to figure things out on our own. It might have been nice for some direction. I feel like a free-floater sometimes, you know?"

"Well, not really. I could do with a little less direction."

"Sounds like we grew up at two different extremes."

"Guess so." I ran my finger down a deep groove in the plank, stopping right before a nail. "What are you planning to do with that biology degree?"

"Oh, you know, just single-handedly save the planet." Isaac smirked and plucked a pebble which quickly sank into the water.

"Nice, remind me to make you a cape." I leaned toward him and whispered. "I can get you some green tights too."

"I think I'll pass on that offer. But seriously, to answer your question, I've been thinking about going into environmental policy."

"That sounds like a good idea."

Isaac handed me a red fishing rod. "I want to see you do this." He placed the bait bucket between us with an audible thud. I removed the plastic lid and lifted a writhing worm from the moist dirt.

"Poor little guy." I held up the creature and observed him wiggle between my fingers.

"Oh, you're not going to get all mushy on me, are you?"

"No, I like to comfort my victims before I kill them."

"Is that why you brought me out here?" Isaac asked, darting his eyes as if pretending to look for an escape route.

"You're the one who brought me out here. Okay enough, Isaac, here goes." I pushed the hook neatly through the midsection of the worm and cast my line deep into the water.

"Well done. I'm impressed." Isaac smiled and baited his hook.

"As you should be. I'm full of surprises." I leaned forward and slid my hand into the water, loosening the dirt from my fingers. Isaac pushed the bait bucket behind him, leaving the space between us open.

"Look, Isaac, to the left," I whispered. A white egret, partially hidden by the beige marsh grass, rubbed his long beak against its back.

"Yes, that's perfect."

The egret continued to groom itself until the breeze rustling the grass distracted it, and the bird flew away.

I closed my eyes and tilted my face toward the sun. When I opened them, I saw Isaac watching me. I smiled.

"Hey, wait!" I pointed to the surface of the water as the line vibrated, creating small ripples. "I think you've got something."

"I do; hold on." Isaac pulled up on the rod and reeled in a small, striped bass.

"Well done, you could feed a family of four on that," I joked. "Four mice, I mean."

"Nice one, Gwyn." Isaac held up the fish. "He's a little guy. Let's return him." Isaac removed the fish and released it into the water.

"Yeah, he deserves to grow up a little more." I leaned forward and propped my elbows on my knees. I gazed at Isaac as he pulled out another worm. "I can tell you love it here—at this river, I mean."

"I do. I like the quiet. It makes me feel hopeful."

"Hopeful?"

"Yeah, that there's still a place where things are as simple as a blue heron providing for her young."

"Yes, hope," I said softly. I reeled in my fishing line to find a half-eaten worm. I set the rod down next to me and stared at the water.

"Have things gotten better with your aunt?"

"Not really." I turned to look at Isaac. "It's like, in my mind, I feel as if I'm screaming for her to understand what I want, what I need, but then when the words leave my mouth, I feel as if—" I paused to gather my thoughts—"as if I'm just whispering through water."

After all the anger and resentment, I still longed for her approval and her love, and those conflicting feelings tormented me. I wanted nothing more than for Aunt Delia to understand that my choice to leave was not a rejection of my family. She tried to protect me from acting on the same fierce independence that I admired in her. My aunt, the one person I was terrified to confront, was the one who I most wanted to hear me.

The tears rose that I had hoped desperately to suppress. I turned away from him and let my hair fall to cover my cheek. Isaac wrapped his arm around my waist and pulled me close to him. This time he did not remove his hand.

Isaac's fishing lure bobbed on the surface of the water as I allowed myself to be embraced by the beautiful, enveloping silence.

13
SORTING

It seems to me we can never give up longing and wishing while we are thoroughly alive. — *George Eliot*

The sensation of Isaac's fingertips against my side lingered as I drove home from the river. Just the thought of his name prompted a chill to run the length of my arms, which amplified the pulse in my wrists. The human heartbeat fascinated me. A rhythm that occurs all day, every day, but we don't feel it until we focus our attention. I've experienced crushes before, but no person had ever made me feel like this.

Despite traveling the same roads as I had since childhood, each turn seemed unfamiliar. The world was different somehow. I noticed the gentle movement of the clouds, the sparrows bathing in water-filled ditches, and the snap of wind in my hair as I leaned toward the open car window. Consumed by my heightened senses, I forgot to turn on the radio, which I didn't realize until I pulled into my driveway.

As I opened the side door to the house, the aroma of my aunt's baked goods filled the kitchen. Muffin tins lined every surface of the room.

"Is this all for the church bazaar?" I asked.

"Yes, they are." Aunt Delia rinsed a bowl in the sink. "Don't touch anything. I have a system." Aunt Delia wiped her hands on an apron. "Those are sugar-free for the people with diabetes." Aunt Delia pointed to trays on the counter above the dishwasher. "Those over there are for people with nut allergies, low-fat ones on top of the refrigerator, and the regular recipe muffins are in the oven."

"Wow, you know how to make a buck, Aunt Delia, taking advantage of people's illnesses." I smiled, awaiting her reaction to my sarcasm.

"Gwyn, that was uncalled for. This is to raise money for the preschool." She shook her hands dry and gave a sly smile. "I can't help it if I know what I am doing."

"Well, anything for the kids," I said, returning the smile. Lately, every conversation with my aunt seemed to end in an argument.

"Baking has consumed most of my time today, so Uncle Beckett is going to take you out for pizza."

"That sounds great. I'll go up and change." I left the kitchen relieved that I would not have to make small talk with her over dinner.

"Oh, Gwyn, you smell like a swamp." Aunt Delia waved her hand in front of her nose.

"I took a walk by the river after work," I said, my voice cracking a little.

"Did you fall in?" She turned to look at me.

"Uh, not exactly." I had fallen for something, but not the river. "Tell Uncle Beckett I'll be right down."

I turned away so Aunt Delia would not see my giddy grin and ran upstairs to my bedroom.

UNCLE BECKETT and I slipped into one of the dimly lit booths at Sal's. A Tiffany lamp hung above each table with the name of an

Italian city spelled out in colored glass. We were sitting under *Verona*, which seemed fitting considering my recent circumstances. I hoped my fate was written differently than Shakespeare's star-crossed lovers, their whole lives altered by a misdirected letter.

"Hey, Mr. James, welcome back, and Gwyn, looking good." Our waiter's eyes traveled from my face to my waist and back again.

"Hey, yourself, Sal Junior." Uncle Beckett nudged my shin with his foot.

"Um, thanks, Sal." I pretended to study the menu so I would not have to look at him. Sal was an untamable flirt, and one of those guys who looked thirty-five in high school and would continue to look thirty-five well into old age. His father owned the restaurant, and Sal seemed to work every shift, making him unavoidable.

"Now that you've graduated, call me, and we'll go out sometime." Sal Junior winked at me.

I quickly turned my eyes to the table. "I don't think so."

"That's just too bad. I could have given my favorite customer free pizza for life." Sal rested his hand on Uncle Beckett's shoulder.

"My girl is going to school in Boston." Uncle Beckett smiled at me. "I really doubt she'll have time for either of us."

"Hey, it was worth a try. Okay, so what'll it be tonight?"

"We want a large pizza, one side with onions and green peppers, right, Gwyn?"

I nodded.

"And the other side with pepperoni," Uncle Beckett said. "We'll have two Cokes as well."

Uncle Beckett closed his menu and handed it to Sal Junior.

"No prob. I'll be right back." Sal Junior turned and slumped toward the kitchen. A rip in the back of his jeans exposed his Santa Claus boxers.

"That boy—" Uncle Beckett shook his head. "His poor father. Sal Senior's daughter finished a degree in accounting last year, but that one, I think he'll be waiting tables for the rest of his life."

"Maybe one day, his flirting will work, and he'll meet a girl who will be happy to marry a career waiter with an affinity for holiday underwear."

"Gwyn, you are something else."

"I get that from you, Uncle." I smiled.

I have eaten at Sal's Restaurant practically every week since it opened twelve years ago. My uncle and I commemorated every childhood celebration within these wood-paneled walls. Aunt Delia found Sal's overly common. She preferred the quiet ambiance of The River's Inn, which served her favorite crab bisque with a seaside view.

Because of Aunt Delia's dislike for the ordinary, I always had two birthday parties. One hosted by my aunt, to which only women were invited. She served lunch on her fine china and cloth napkins that matched the fresh-cut flowers from our yard. It took my friends several years to understand the difference between a dinner fork and salad fork. The other party occurred here, with Uncle Beckett, a few friends, my dad—who was secretly invited by my uncle—and twelve large pizzas.

I stared at the map of Italy on the wall above our booth, watching the black line of the country's border expand and contract in my field of vision. Uncle Beckett explained his latest quest to find a rare book, but my mind drifted. Being this distracted was so unlike me.

I did not hear Sal Junior approach the table. "Am I interrupting something?" he asked, sliding our drinks onto the table with a flourish.

"Uh, no, we were just talking," I said.

"About me, I hope." He winked at me a second time. "Your pizza will be up shortly." His gold bracelet caught the light from the Tiffany lamp, causing a yellow-white beam to dance on the wall.

We waited until Sal Junior was a safe distance away before speaking again.

"Gwyn, I wanted to talk to you about something. Nana Lola broke her hip yesterday."

"Oh, I'm sorry, Uncle."

Nana Lola and Papa Clive, Uncle Beckett's parents, were well into their eighties. I had not seen them for several years, but I remembered how nice they'd always been to me. On holidays, they sent me a card with a five-dollar bill and before it became hard for them to travel, they attended my school plays.

Nana Lola's parents were Spanish immigrants and Papa Clive's were Irish. I decided that Uncle Beckett's Spanish heritage must have given him an exotic look in his youth. Now, he was almost entirely gray, leaving only small traces of rich black hair. Nana Lola and Papa Clive's parents ended up settling in New Orleans and attended the same Catholic church—that's how Nana Lola and Papa Clive met. Growing up, I never knew my uncle to adhere to any organized religion, but I am not sure if his parents were aware of that. Papa Clive considered himself an Irish literature expert. He named my uncle after an up-and-coming writer, Samuel Beckett. Papa Clive said he just knew Beckett would be famous one day.

"It's okay. These things happen when you age." Uncle Beckett shook his head. "I am leaving this Sunday for Delaware. I need to help my parents move into an assisted living community. With my father's diabetes and my mother's arthritis, they can't stay in our family house anymore."

"I understand. How long are you going to stay?" I swirled the straw around in my glass.

"I think I'll be there at least three weeks. My mother is still in the hospital, so my father and I will have to decide what furniture they want to move. We're not going to worry about selling the house right now."

Uncle Beckett patted my hand. "Gwynnie, it's only a few weeks. I promise I'll be back in time to drive you to college. I want to be there when you move in."

"I know you will, Uncle. Hey, wait a second, you're going to miss my birthday." I jutted my bottom lip into a childish pout, attempting to make him laugh. It always made me uncomfortable to see him sad.

"You're going to be eighteen, an adult, so that pouting won't work," he teased and waved his finger at me.

"Okay, but who am I going to talk to when Aunt Delia is driving me crazy?"

"You can always come talk to me," Sal Junior said with a trill in his voice. Once again, I had not seen him approach our table. The man was way too stealthy. I rolled my eyes, giving him the full measure of my annoyance.

"Well, at any rate, here's the best pizza this side of the Mississippi." He set the pizza tray on the silver stand in the middle of the table.

"Can't argue with you there," Uncle Beckett said.

Sal Junior moved on to another table of customers. Uncle Beckett and I each lifted a slice of pizza, forming a connecting line of cheese from the pizza tray to our plates.

"I'll be sure to call you. The time will go by just like that." Uncle Beckett snapped his fingers. "My friend Keith, who works at the *Tribune*, is going to open the bookshop in the afternoons and on Saturdays. Justine will be there on the weekday mornings. I don't want to miss out on the summer tourists."

"I hope everything goes well." I raised a slice to my mouth and breathed in the glorious aroma of crushed red pepper and tomato sauce. "Maybe lifelong free pizza wouldn't be a bad thing. Except eventually we could only be moved with a forklift."

I bit into it and held the flavors on my tongue before beginning to chew, savoring the warm combination of cheese, sauce, and crust.

After finishing my first piece of pizza, I reached for another. "Can I ask you something? Something that I've been curious about."

"Sure, what is it?" Uncle Beckett looked up from his own slice.

"Do you remember when you showed me Aunt Delia's paintings?"

"Yes." Leaning over his plate, my uncle peered at me over the thin rim of his glasses.

"Well, you said that you went to London because you lost something." I paused and shifted uncomfortably in my seat. "Um, do you mind me asking what happened?"

Uncle Beckett rubbed his right temple.

"Not something, Gwynnie, someone," he said quietly.

"You don't have to tell me if it's private. I didn't mean to pry." I gestured with my hands to emphasize that it was okay if he didn't feel like talking about it.

"No, no, I don't mind telling you. Actually, it's something I wanted to tell you one day. Several years before I met your aunt, I was engaged to another woman."

Uncle Beckett stopped and breathed deeply.

"I met her at a friend's Christmas party in graduate school. She—Catherine—worked as a nurse at the veterans' hospital. Her beauty and intelligence took my breath away..."

Uncle Beckett trailed off. He turned toward the window, and his eyes seemed to follow a mom pushing a stroller down the sidewalk. Several silent moments passed. Once the mother and stroller were out of view, his focus returned to the table.

"I was so much in love with her."

"What happened?" I asked quietly.

"Catherine died in a car accident while driving to her parent's house. She wanted to help her mom address the wedding invitations. A truck crossed the centerline, hitting her head-on, and that was it."

"Oh, God." My eyes were wide, and I covered my mouth with my hand. "I'm so sorry. I never knew."

"It's okay." Uncle Beckett patted my hand. "I don't talk about it much. Hey, don't look so sad. It was a long time ago."

"But you loved her, and she was just taken away."

"That's why I had to leave. I couldn't bear being in Delaware. Before I left, her parents returned the engagement ring to me. They were so supportive, but I lost touch with them over time."

Uncle Beckett picked up his glass, took a sip of soda, and swallowed hard.

"The ring was a platinum setting," he said. "I spent months saving up the money. I never sold it, but sadly, over the years, the ring disappeared somehow."

"Disappeared? What do you mean?" Fully engrossed in his story, I placed my forearms on the table and leaned forward.

"I had given Catherine the ring in a tin heart-shaped box, which her parents also returned. From then on, I kept the ring in the box. I took it with me to London and brought it with me when I moved here. But somehow, in the move from the bookshop apartment to our current house, it vanished. I searched everywhere but never found it."

I sat in stunned silence. My thoughts flashed to the heart-shaped container I found in Aunt Delia's shoebox. The container I never opened because I thought it inconsequential. Why would Aunt Delia have taken Catherine's ring?

"Gwyn, are you okay? You're mighty quiet."

I nervously tucked hair behind my ear. "Yeah, um, does anyone else know you kept the ring?"

"No. You are the only person I've told." Uncle Beckett wiped his mouth with a napkin. "I wish I could find it again. It's something I would have given to you."

"To me? Why?"

"Because you're my girl." Uncle Beckett smiled and touched my nose with his finger.

UNCLE BECKETT HAD ALWAYS SEEMED to carry an air of melancholy with him, and now I knew why. That night, after returning home from the restaurant, I rummaged through my closet to find Aunt Delia's hidden shoebox. I sat down in the small space, forging an opening between my hanging clothes to allow me to sit upright. I combed through the box and found the heart-shaped tin. I removed the lid to find the tin stuffed with a small white cloth, which I took out and placed in the palm of my hand. When I originally discovered the tin box, I thought it was empty. The cloth had prevented me from hearing the contents when I shook it.

I reverently unfolded the cloth to reveal the most exquisite ring I had ever seen. The diamond, flanked by two dark blue sapphires, appeared to be about a carat. Denise's Aunt Maureen owned a jewelry store, and she taught us about gems. Aunt Maureen claimed a boy was no good if he tried to pass off a fake stone for a real one. Today, I could finally put my skills to work in the real world. I slipped the ring onto my left hand and observed the diamond refract light on the closet ceiling. My mind wandered to Catherine, the last person to wear this ring.

Thoughts raced faster than I could harness them. My aunt and uncle both had been in love with other people before meeting one another. Had they married each other out of desperation or social pressure? Did they love each other at all? I imagined Aunt Delia, newly married, finding the heart-shaped container as she packed her husband's clothing. I imagined her hands begin to shake as she compared the size of Catherine's ring to her own and in jealousy or heartache, she hid it among the artifacts of her own lost love.

The diamond must be returned to Uncle Beckett; I had no right to keep it. I opened my desk drawer and pulled out a pen and paper and composed a letter to my uncle.

> Uncle Beckett,
> I found the heart-shaped box last week when I was looking through a box of old pictures, but I never opened it. I didn't know it held something precious until you told me Catherine's story. The ring is found. All is not lost.
> Love you,
> Gwynnie

I decided to place the ring and the letter in Uncle Beckett's glove compartment. After every visit to the gas station, he would write the car's current mileage in a small notebook he kept there, so I knew he would eventually find it. I didn't have the words to give him the ring in person.

Sunday morning, I offered to carry Uncle Beckett's luggage to the car, and in the process, I placed the heart-shaped box in its temporary home, waiting to be found.

14
ISAAC

*D*anny and Denise chatted so enthusiastically on our drive to Isaac's that they did not notice I hadn't spoken most of the trip. I drove, and Denise sat in the passenger seat while Danny spread out in the back seat. They discussed their most recent plans to attend the local community college for two years, then transfer together to a university in California. Danny handed Denise the college catalog through the space between the two front seats, hitting me in the arm and causing me to jerk the steering wheel.

"Hey, sorry, Gwyn. I didn't mean to make you swerve," Danny said.

"Huh, what?" I responded absentmindedly.

"I'm. Sorry. I. Hit. Your. Arm." Danny tapped the back of my seat as if he was playing the drums. "Hey, what's with you anyway? You're acting spacey."

Denise shot me a sly smile. "I know what's wrong with her."

"It's this Isaac guy, isn't it? So, what gives?" Danny wore a ridiculous Fourth of July hat that was so tall, it scraped the ceiling of the car and prevented him from fully turning his head.

"What do you mean?" I asked, trying to evade his question.

"You know what he means," Denise said. "Come on, you like him. You're like, together now, right?"

"We are not together. Not exactly anyway." I absentmindedly pushed my curly hair away from my shoulder. I had made two long braids on the sides of my head and clipped them together at the nape of my neck. My dad always told me my hair looked pretty that way. It's times like these I wish I saw my dad more often. He called himself a "free spirit". Whenever his motorcycle and the open road called him, he was gone. Part of me wished he would get re-married, that might cause him to settle down in one place.

"Oh, my God, you are together," Denise said, the excitement in her voice escalating. "Has he kissed you yet?"

Danny leaned forward through the console as if afraid he would miss something.

"No, he hasn't, Denise."

"But he will, you know he will, and you back there—" She turned to look at Danny. "You, be nice tonight."

"What? What am I gonna do?" Danny answered defensively.

"Oh, you know good and well," Denise scolded. "No teasing, no embarrassing comments. You remember what happened at Andrea's party? You locked Andrea and the guy she liked in the bathroom together, and everyone called her Farts for the rest of the year."

"Yeah, so hilarious! How was I supposed to know when Andrea got nervous that she passed gas?" Danny leaned back chuckling to himself, then snapped forward. "But this is Gwyn; I wouldn't do that to her. She's like my sister."

"Just know I'm watching you." Denise shot Danny a teacher-like glare.

"Okay, guys, we're here," I said. "Deep breaths."

Isaac was not kidding when he said thirty family members would be attending. Dozens of vehicles filled the driveway, so we pulled onto the grass next to a large Dodge Ram.

Isaac must have been waiting nearby for our arrival, because before I even turned off the ignition, he stood waiting to open my door.

I stepped out of the car. "Thank you."

Isaac leaned toward me and whispered in my ear. "I'm glad you're here."

I could feel blood rush into my cheeks. I turned away so Denise and Danny would not see me blush.

"So, aren't you going to introduce us?" I heard Danny ask from behind me.

"Um, yeah." I turned to my friends who were standing in front of my car. "Isaac, this is my best friend, Denise, and her boyfriend, Danny."

"Nice to meet you." Isaac shook their hands.

"I hope it's okay that we're here," Denise said, sounding apologetic.

"It's no problem. I'll warn you, though, my family will be all over you in a second. They are, what can I say, friendly. But we've got lots of food."

"As long as there's food, I'm good." Danny smiled.

"Alright then, follow me." Isaac grabbed my hand, encouraging me to walk next to him.

I thought about wriggling my hand away from his grip, embarrassed at such intimacy in the presence of my friends, but I decided I liked the sensation of his hand against mine. The connection made me feel seen, though I tried to ignore mental images of Denise and Danny whispering behind me.

"Are you nervous?" Isaac asked me quietly.

"A little."

"Don't worry. My family will love you." Isaac smiled. Only a handful of guys I graduated with were eye-level with me, most were shorter. It was nice to be able to gaze up at Isaac.

"I like those." He pointed to the portraits of James Dean and Marilyn Monroe.

"Oh, my leggings, thanks. My mom hates them."

"Well, I think they're cool."

A large canvas canopy trimmed with red, white, and blue lights, sat in the field behind Isaac's house. Several middle-aged adults danced to seventies' rock classics blaring from the stereo. We stood in a line a few feet from the canopy as if we were watching a carnival act.

"Your family looks like fun," Danny said. "Let's join 'em." He pulled Denise by the hand, and they began dancing, throwing themselves into the beat of Led Zeppelin.

I stood, holding Isaac's hand, peering into a world so markedly different from mine. I heard the soft thump of a volleyball contacting flesh, followed by jubilant yelps. Four men, two in bright Hawaiian shirts, were engaged in an animated discussion, one excitedly waving his hands as he talked. Children chased a Border Collie around the card tables, almost collapsing several of them.

"Overwhelming, isn't it?" Isaac said.

"Yeah, I couldn't imagine my family ever throwing a party like this. I could see my mom having fun, but for Aunt Delia, this would be enough to cause a coronary." I paused. "But shouldn't you be used to all this by now?"

"You would think. I'm not the loud type, I guess, unlike your friend Danny over there." Isaac pointed to Danny, who attempted to surf on a folding chair with one foot on the seat and the other on the back rim.

I laughed. "He wasted no time joining in."

"Hey, I want you to meet my sister." Isaac waved to a beautiful girl, in a soft orange halter dress, who glided out of the back door of the ranch house. She accompanied Isaac's mother, who carried a large tray of fruit and cheese. His sister motioned to the food table, and we wandered over to meet them.

"Veronica, this is Gwyn." Isaac put his arm loosely around my shoulder.

I reached out to shake Veronica's hand.

"It's great to meet you," Veronica said, flashing a radiant smile. "You're actually the first girl Isaac's brought home."

Veronica had dark brown hair that fell in a neat line half-way down her back. Her bangs were cut bluntly above her brow line, framing her beautiful, creamy skin.

"Don't start that, Vee."

"I'm not trying to embarrass you." Veronica reached up and pinched Isaac's right cheek. "It's just that she must be special if you brought her home, little brother."

"Hey, baby," said a dark-complected young man with kind eyes. He slid next to Veronica and wrapped his arm around her waist.

"Hey, Chris." Veronica kissed the man on the cheek. "This is Gwyn; she's with my brother."

I gave Chris a slight wave and a half-smile. He exuded this dignified confidence that you couldn't help but be attracted to. At my small high school, the interracial couples never lasted long. It was hard to fight against the status quo; most either had to escape town or give up trying.

"Good, so now I'll have someone to endure these Quigley parties with. Nice to have you around." Chris bumped his shoulder against mine. "Vee, I told your dad I would help him with the grill." He kissed Veronica and waved goodbye to us.

I attempted to make small talk, which wasn't my strong suit. "He seems very nice. Isaac told me you got married in Aruba. That sounds amazing, Veronica."

"So amazing," Veronica said. "I would suggest eloping to anybody. Especially with this group."

She opened her arms and gestured to the crowd surrounding us. "Our parents are throwing Chris and me a reception on the eighteenth. You should come with Isaac." She eyed her brother. "You've asked her, right, Isaac?"

"Vee, you're worse than Mom. We haven't exactly talked about it, but I planned to." Isaac turned toward me. "Do you want to come?"

"I don't think I can say no at this point." I laughed. I put my arm around his waist and squeezed him. "But, I don't really have anything to wear."

"Don't worry about anything," Veronica said. "I still have several formals hanging in my closet here. You are welcome to one. Before you leave tonight, we'll get it taken care of."

Veronica turned as her mom brought another tray to the table, this one filled with mounds of cookies. "Mom, I invited Gwyn to the reception," she said enthusiastically.

"That's great, sweetie. Hey Gwyn, it's good to see you again." Mrs. Quigley startled me with a hug. "I'm glad you brought her, Isaac."

"Thanks, Mom, me too." Isaac twisted the toe of his shoe in the grass.

"Gwyn, Isaac said you were a vegetarian, so we made sure we grilled some kabobs with no meat."

"Wow, thanks. No one does that for me at home."

"It's no problem. We feel like if someone has strong convictions about something, it should be honored."

"I really appreciate it, Mrs. Quigley."

She nodded and smiled. "Son, why don't you take Gwyn and show her the horses? Dinner won't be ready for a little while."

"You wanna go?" Isaac asked.

"Sounds great, but what about Denise and Danny?"

"Your friends are fine. My sisters are taking care of them," Mrs. Quigley said. Isaac's mom turned to indicate a group of people doing the limbo to "Walk This Way."

"If I didn't know better, I would think your friends are related to me," Mrs. Quigley added, patting Isaac on the shoulder.

The noise from the party muffled as we crossed the backyard toward the fenced pasture. A freshly painted red barn stood at the far end, its large doors standing open to reveal bales of hay stacked like a staircase.

"Okay, when you feed them, lay your palm out flat, don't bend your fingers." Isaac placed a carrot in my hand. Soon, a chocolate-colored quarter horse approached the fence where we stood.

"Hey, girl," Isaac said. He began rubbing the horse behind the ears and kissing her muzzle. "Gwyn, this is CoCo Chanel. My sister named her."

"Hey, CoCo." I held out my hand, and the horse took the carrot, her tongue rough against my skin. I glanced up to see another horse approaching us.

"This one is Father Rigsby. He gets a little jealous, don't you, boy?"

"Father Rigsby?"

The horse neighed, exposing his rectangular teeth.

"Yeah, my mom named him after a priest in one of those British comedies she watches."

I allowed the horse to smell me. "He's beautiful. What kind is he?"

"He's an Appaloosa. Aren't you, boy?" Isaac held out a carrot that the horse quickly ate. "Maybe, sometime, I'll take you out riding."

"I'd like that." I rubbed Father Rigsby behind the ears.

Isaac plucked a dandelion from the fence edge. He gently blew the seeds into the evening air.

"It's really sweet of your sister to invite me to the reception and let me borrow a dress," I said.

"Veronica liked you; I could tell. She's one of the most genuine people I know. I just wished I could have asked you first." Isaac ran his fingers through his thick hair. "I warned you, I'm not used to this dating thing."

"And why is that? I would have thought plenty of girls would be lined up to be with you."

My heart rate accelerated. Every word squeaked out, awkward to my ears. I mindlessly rubbed CoCo, who had positioned herself in front of me. The horse flared her nostrils and released a satisfied exhale. She shook her head, letting her mane chase away a fly that buzzed about her head.

"That's just it," Isaac said. "I feel like most girls, at least the ones who ever showed interest in me, were always trying to be someone they weren't, and I didn't want to deal with that." Isaac tucked a stray hair behind my ear. "I wasn't sure at first, but when I took a chance and came to see you at work, I could tell."

"Tell what?" I asked.

"I could tell you were most comfortable when you were just being yourself, and I like who you are."

"I like you, too, Isaac." The corners of my lips lifted to a shy grin.

We stood in silence for what felt like minutes, but most likely only ten seconds. CoCo broke the stillness as she loudly snorted, threw her head back, and whinnied.

"I guess she approves," I added with a laugh.

"Smart horse." Isaac picked up one last carrot, which CoCo promptly gobbled.

"You know, your sister's reception is three days after my birthday."

"I'll have to keep that in mind." Isaac grinned. "If I forget to tell you later, thanks for coming tonight." He slid next to me and wrapped his arm around my waist. I rested my head against his shoulder.

"You've already thanked me."

"Well, it bears repeating then."

"In that case, you're welcome."

Coco let out a dramatic snort as if she agreed. The horse nudged my hand that was resting on the fencepost. I took the hint and rubbed her muzzle.

"Denise asked about us on the drive here." As soon as the words left my mouth, a knot formed in my throat. I kept my gaze on Coco. I knew if I looked at Isaac, the knot would grow.

"Oh really?" Isaac's eyebrows shot up. "What did she ask?"

I swallowed hard. "Denise asked if we were together. How would you answer that question?"

His fingertips tapped my side, like when someone tapped on a desk while thinking of a response. "That's a big word, *together*."

"Yeah, I guess it is." I wrapped my arm around his back.

We stood in close silence. I turned my eyes to the horizon as the sun drifted downward, with the purple spray of yellow light filling the expanse above the barn.

AFTER DINNER, Mrs. Quigley distributed quilts and lawn chairs to her guests. We meandered to the edge of the property overlooking the river. Isaac's two youngest cousins ran between the adults with quilts draped over their shoulders like superhero capes. His aunts began to sing their own rendition of "Shall We Gather at the River." Once we reached the property's edge, Isaac laid down our quilt next to Danny and Denise.

"Thanks for having us, man. Your family is great." Danny tore open a bag of pretzels.

"No problem." Isaac put his arm around my shoulder and squeezed. "I'm glad I got to meet some of Gwyn's friends too."

Denise leaned back and winked at me, making sure Isaac didn't see her.

"Yeah, we like her. She's okay," Danny teased.

"Danny, you're not from around here, right?" Isaac leaned forward and propped his forearms on his knees and looked at Danny.

"No, I'm from Pasadena, California."

"That's awesome," Isaac said. "My mom would be jealous. She always joked she wanted to travel to the West Coast in a Winnebago and live out her hippie fantasies."

"Now that wasn't a joke, son."

Isaac jumped at the sound of his mother's voice.

Mrs. Quigley placed her hands on her son's shoulders and laughed.

"Sorry, Mom, I didn't see you back there."

Mrs. Quigley tousled Isaac's hair. He winced and childishly batted away her hand. She turned her attention to me.

"I wanted to chat with Gwyn. I haven't gotten a chance to talk with her much this evening." She sat down next to me.

"Sure, I'd like that." My heart raced. I realized this might be my only chance tonight to find out more information about my aunt.

"Son, why don't you get us some drinks from the cooler?" Mrs. Quigley asked.

Denise jumped up, and Danny followed her lead.

"We'll go with you," Denise said. "All that dancing made me thirsty." She gave me a nod of encouragement before following the boys.

"I'm really glad you came, honey," Mrs. Quigley said. "It must have been fate that you delivered those flowers to our house."

I smiled and nodded.

"So, Gwyn, tell me a little about yourself. Isaac said you are going to Massachusetts to study graphic design; that's wonderful."

"Yes, that's right." I plucked a buttercup from the grass and twisted the stem between my fingers. "Um, what would you like to know, Mrs. Quigley?"

"First, call me Brenda." She patted my leg.

"Brenda," I said.

"Well, why not start with telling me about your parents."

"My mom's a receptionist at the hospital. Her name is Trisha, Trisha Madison."

I searched for signs in Mrs. Quigley's expression that indicated she recognized Mom's name. She just smiled and nodded for me to continue. I bet she was someone who would smile at a stranger in an elevator and by the time the doors opened, she would know the person's life story.

"My parents got divorced when I was two," I said. "My dad's an electrician. He lives near Richmond, but he travels a lot." I took a deep breath and stared at the face of the buttercup. "Mom and I moved in with my aunt and uncle after my parents divorced."

"That would be nice to have all of those family members under the same roof."

"Yeah." I twirled the buttercup stem between my fingers.

"Who are your aunt and uncle?"

I breathed deeply. If I said their names quickly, it would be less painful, like ripping off a Band-Aid.

"Delia and Beckett James. My uncle owns the bookshop downtown."

Mrs. Quigley's bright eyes noticeably dimmed. She looked away from me and rubbed her forehead before turning back around.

"What's your aunt's maiden name?" She asked leaning forward to massage her left ankle.

"Strickland. Do you know her?"

"No, um…" Mrs. Quigley seemed to be searching for the right words. "I mean, she was an acquaintance." She interlaced her fingers and rubbed her thumbs against each other.

Her uneasiness prompted me to change the subject, and frankly, I was becoming uncomfortable as well.

"I really wanted to thank you for having me and my friends over tonight. It's been really fun."

"You're quite welcome." The brightness returned to Mrs. Quigley's eyes. "Isaac said you were a wonderful artist. I would love to see some of your work."

"He's exaggerating. I have a lot more to learn, but I'll be happy to bring my sketchbook over next time I come."

"Sounds good." Mrs. Quigley called to her son and my friends, motioning them over. "The fireworks are starting. You don't want to miss this!"

Isaac laid down on the quilt next to me, propping up on his elbows. Denise handed me a soda and sat down next to Danny. We viewed the metallic bursts produce trails of light in the sky. I leaned my head back and allowed the streaks of color to blanket my senses mingling with the sounds of vibrant applause echoing in my ears.

15
DETAILS

Danny snored lightly in the backseat of my Volkswagen as we drove home to Riverbend. The limbo had apparently exhausted him. He looked ridiculous, sleeping in a fetal position with his head wedged in the fold of the seat. Danny had to be a foot taller than my car was wide.

"You and Isaac, so cute." Denise grinned, biting her lower lip. "I'm taking credit for this, you know."

"What are you talking about?" I asked.

"If it wasn't for me, you wouldn't have met him in the first place. I came up with the fake flower order. You can't deny that."

"Okay, I'll give you that one, but the actual dating thing, I think I did alright by myself."

"So, you admit it," Denise said, clapping her hands. "You are dating! Has he kissed you yet?"

I gripped the steering wheel. "That is none of your business."

"Yes, it is, I'm your best friend."

Danny mumbled something incoherent between snores. We both laughed.

"He's your boyfriend," I teased. "Danny really enjoyed himself tonight, huh?"

"You're evading the subject. We were talking about you and Isaac." Denise gestured for me to speak.

"No, he hasn't kissed me yet, Denise."

"But he will, and I better be the first one you call."

"Who else?" I smiled and tapped the wheel.

"Oh, I almost forgot. What did Mrs. Quigley say when you talked to her?"

"It was a little strange. She said she only knew my aunt as an acquaintance, but it's what she didn't say that mattered."

"What do you mean?"

"Well, for one, Mrs. Quigley wouldn't look at me after I asked about Aunt Delia, and then she hesitated before she answered. Come to think of it—at first, she started to say she didn't know Aunt Delia."

"Sounds like there's something more to that story, Gwyn."

"I know, but I couldn't press it. It seemed like the wrong time. I don't know, I guess I should just—" I paused, slowing to make a turn.

"You guess you should just what?" Denise asked.

"That I should just drop it. I don't want to mess things up with Isaac. I really like him, and I don't want this to all blow up in my face."

"Yeah, you're probably right." Denise pulled down the visor and pressed her cheekbones, "God, I look rough," she mumbled to herself.

"And if I stay with Isaac, whatever the story is, it will probably come out on its own, right?"

"If you date long enough, eventually Mrs. Quigley and your aunt will have to meet." Denise shivered. "Will you be ready for that?"

"Thanks a lot. Now you are going to give me nightmares. Let me just get through the summer first."

"Good, let's change the subject. I don't want to think any more about what happens when your aunt finds out I'm aiding and abetting for you."

A light rain began to fall. I turned on the wipers to the lowest setting and listened to the intermittent sound of rubber scraping against glass.

Denise was right, if I stayed with Isaac, the truth would be unavoidable. Eventually our families would meet, and then what? If I could only hold out until the end of the summer, the truth would be easier to face several states away. I had to put the thought out of my mind and deal with the present.

"Okay, so now you'll have to help me figure out how to get to Veronica's wedding reception without Aunt Delia finding out."

My thoughts wandered to the garment bag which I had laid neatly in the trunk of my car. Veronica insisted I try on five dresses before leaving the house that night. I finally chose the most feminine dress I had ever considered wearing, and I loved it. The floor-length halter dress was cotton with a slight sheen to the fabric. Several large red poppies with dark black centers were spaced over the white bodice. I needed to locate the proper shoes, but between my mom's closet and Denise's flair for fashion, I knew I was covered.

"Let me figure that one out," Denise said, rubbing her hand together. "I'm good at devious plans. When is the big event?"

"The eighteenth, in two weeks."

"I'll work on it, don't worry. Hey, can you still help me paint my room that weekend, the day after the reception? You're so good at that stuff."

"No problem. We'll work something out. I think I owe you one anyway." I pulled into my driveway, parking my car in its usual space in front of the left garage door. "Hey Danny, it's time to get up. We're here."

I turned and punched Danny in the leg. He sat straight up and fumbled for his ball cap that had fallen on the floorboard.

"Huh, what? Where are we?"

"Gwyn's house," Denise said. "Come on, baby. We've got to drive home now."

Denise motioned for Danny to sit up. He gave her a sleepy smile.

"Gwyn, tell Isaac…" Danny yawned, unfolded his legs, and slid out of the car. "Tell Isaac that the party was great; that he's great, whatever, you know what I mean."

"I should be thanking y'all," I said. "It means a lot that you would come with me."

"That's what friends are for, right?" Denise said. "And anyway, we made a pact in fifth grade, you can't break that." She smiled and blew me a kiss before climbing into her car. Danny waved through the passenger window.

When we were ten, Denise and I pooled our Christmas money to buy "best friends" necklaces. From each silver chain hung a pendant that, when matched together, made a complete heart. We made a pact that no distance could separate our friendship. I knew that even hundreds of miles apart, we would be okay. I think we have proven ourselves by now.

THAT NIGHT IN MY DREAMS, I found myself sitting at the dining room table, which was fully dressed in white linens, my aunt's fine china, and silver candlesticks. But the table, centered on the wooden planks of the pier, sat in the center of the wooden pier where Isaac and I fished for the first time. My aunt, at least seven feet tall, sat across from Mrs. Quigley, who wore a teal bridesmaid's dress. They stared at each other, eyes bulging. Isaac sat across from me; strangely, he had no mouth, and then I realized neither did I. The water rose through the openings between each wood plank, chilling my bare feet.

"Gwyn," I heard my mom whisper loudly, jarring me out of sleep. "Gwyn, are you awake?"

Mom rapped on my bedroom door. She pushed the door slightly open and peered into my room. I rolled over in bed and glanced at my clock.

"Mom, it's five A.M." I turned back toward the door and rubbed my eyes.

"I know. I just got home and I'm dying to know how the party went." Mom came in and laid down on her side, facing me on the bed. She was still dressed in scrubs, with her blond hair piled on her head and held in place with bobby pins. She propped herself up on her elbow. "Come on Gwyn, I'm your mother." She pointed her thumb to her chest for emphasis. "Give me some details."

"God, Mom, you're worse than Denise. You're acting like a teenager." I rolled over so my back was on her.

"Come on, I've been at work all night. I need to hear something happy." Mom put her hands on my side and rolled me over.

I sat up. "Okay, fine. We had a great time. Isaac is really nice."

"Tell me about him. What's he like?"

"Mom, it's so early." I rubbed my eyes.

She did not respond but only smiled wider.

I sighed. I knew I would not win this battle.

"Well, he's really sweet and polite. He's a little shy, but that's understandable, because his family's kind of overwhelming. Not like in a bad way; just really friendly. You would have loved them."

"I'm glad you had a good time. You needed a little fun." Mom tucked my hair behind my ear and touched my cheek with her palm.

"Yeah, I guess I did." I smiled at her.

"I did want to talk to you about your birthday," she said enthusiastically. "I thought that since your birthday falls on a Wednesday this year, and Uncle Beckett is out of town, that I would take you to Sal's for dinner."

"That sounds like a good idea. I'd like that."

"And I want you to invite Denise, Danny, and Isaac. I would like to meet him, since I have a feeling—" her voice trailed off.

"A feeling about what?"

Mom smoothed the duvet cover with her hand and grinned at me.

"A feeling that he'll be around for a while, that's all. It's one of those motherly feelings."

"When did you start getting those?" I teased.

"Don't be silly." Mom put her hand over mine. "So, it's okay with you?"

"Sure, I'll ask them. I think it will be fun, and who knows, maybe with Isaac there, I'll finally get Sal Junior off my back."

"Yes, the last thing I want is to have Sal Junior as my son-in-law." Mom let out an audible grunt.

"I can assure you that won't happen. Um, so is Aunt Delia coming too?"

"No, this is just a celebration for us. Plus, you know how she hates eating there."

"Greasy food, greasy tables, greasy regret," I said in my best Aunt Delia voice.

"That's exactly what she says." Mom laughed. "I didn't figure you would be ready to tell her about Isaac anyway. You can try him out on me first."

"Thanks, Mom. You always know."

"That's my job." She touched my nose with her finger. "On a more serious note, your aunt is planning her usual formal birthday luncheon for Thursday. Your cousin Carrie couldn't make it on your actual birthday, so Delia's switching things up. I'm sure she'll want you to invite Denise too."

Carrie was actually my second cousin. Her father, my mom, and Aunt Delia were first cousins, and Carrie and I spent many summers together when we were kids. Both of her parents worked full-time, and she needed a place to stay between summer camps. We both grew up without any siblings, so she made for my makeshift big sister. Carrie was three years older than me, and I had always looked up to her. She taught me how to shave my legs, put on make-up, and tilt my head when a boy kissed me, a skill I soon hoped to put to use. The summer after Carrie graduated from high school, her parents moved to Fredericksburg, and I did not see any of them as much anymore.

"I'm sure it will be really nice," I said. "Aunt Delia always has things so perfect."

"Yes, I'm sure it will. I'm excited I'm off this year for your eighteenth birthday."

"Me too. It will be great."

"Okay, now go back to sleep." Mom leaned and kissed me on the forehead. She stood and tiptoed across the floor, closing my bedroom door behind her. I nestled into my pillow and pulled the sheet over my shoulders, hoping to settle into a happier dream.

16
DAYDREAMS

Isaac did not call me for the next three days, and my anxiety grew with each passing hour. Maybe he realized I wasn't what he wanted, too average-looking and awkward-despite what he said. In my imagination, he visited me again at the florist, bringing a single stem of a daffodil or iris. The flower changed with each daydream. He would pull me close, brushing his lips against mine, but then the image would fade.

I did what I always did when I got nervous—I organized the store. I labeled each drawer according to its contents and systemized the folders on the computer desktop. By four o'clock on Thursday, I had mustered the courage to call Isaac. I dialed the number, but it was Mrs. Quigley who answered.

"Mrs. Quigley? This is Gwyn."

"Yes, hello, dear."

"Would it be okay if I spoke to Isaac?"

"Well, actually he is on his way to see you. He left about fifteen minutes ago."

"He is, really?" My heart began to race.

"Yes, he had been pacing the house since Monday trying to decide when to call you and what to say when he did. I finally got fed up and told him to go visit you at work. My son can be too analytical for his own good."

"I understand, more than you know, Mrs. Quigley."

"Of course, dear. Just promise me to act surprised when he comes. He would be furious with me if he knew I told you." I could hear the smile in her voice. "And it's Brenda."

"Yes, Brenda, I will. See you soon."

"Bye, Gwyn."

I replaced the receiver to the phone base and began to mentally calculate Isaac's arrival. If he left the house fifteen minutes ago, he should be pulling into the back parking lot in ten minutes and walking through the front door one or two minutes later. What to do for twelve agonizing minutes?

Oh, well. There were always pencils to be sharpened.

I did not want Isaac to catch me staring at the window, obviously anticipating his approach, so I concentrated on the pencil shavings as they fell into the trash can. I did not look up until I heard the jingle of the bells attached to the florist door.

Isaac gave me a slight wave. "Hey, Gwyn." He closed the door behind him. The afternoon light shone through the top of the window, and I could see the specks of light dance on the ridges of his curly hair.

"Hey, yourself." I tried to suppress the huge grin emerging on my face. I didn't want to look too eager. "So, why did you stop by?"

"I wanted to see you." He walked to the counter and gripped the edge.

"You did? I was getting worried." I couldn't believe what I had just admitted. I traced a spiral on the countertop with my finger to try to muzzle the feeling of vulnerability.

"About what?" he asked.

"Well, when I didn't hear from you after the party, I thought that—" I paused, trying to allow my thoughts to catch up with my mouth.

"You thought what?"

"That you changed your mind about me, about us," I said in a low voice. Isaac placed his hand over mine, sending a chill up my arm.

"I'm sorry, Gwyn." He squeezed my hand and released. "That's definitely not what I want you to think. I didn't call because, I guess, I couldn't think of what to say. I like you, and I didn't want to say something stupid and screw this up."

His eyes met mine, and I smiled. I noticed he'd had a haircut in the past three days, but his brown curls were still long enough to run my hands through. I resisted the urge. I wanted to lean across the counter and kiss him right there, but he seemed nervous enough already, and Mrs. Jenkins could walk out of the back room at any moment. I breathed deeply and tried to clear my head.

"It's good to know we're—" I couldn't find the right words.

"We're thinking the same way?" he finished.

"Yes." I nodded.

We stood in silence. His hand tightly closed over mine. He wore Birkenstocks and a thick hemp bracelet, which was a shade lighter than his tanned arms.

"I need to ask you something, Isaac."

"Okay." He rubbed his thumb against the back of my hand.

"My birthday is coming up, on the sixteenth. And my mom wanted to take me to Sal's. Denise and Danny are coming, and she wants you to come too."

"Do you want me to come?"

"Yes," I said sheepishly.

"I'll be there. What time?"

"Around six. Is that okay?"

"Yeah." He glanced at the refrigerated case holding the premade rose bouquets. "Maybe if you could get off a little earlier that day, we could hang out before meeting your mom for dinner."

I silently repeated the word *we* in hopes of wrapping my mind around the magnitude of the word.

"I would like that a lot." My heart pounded as if it could bounce right out of my chest. "Since it's my birthday, I'm sure Mrs. Jenkins will let me leave a couple hours early. I'll ask her today."

I looked at Isaac. His smile filled me.

"Then it's a date," Isaac said. He leaned over the counter and kissed my forehead. He slowly released his lips, leaving my skin tingling. "We can go to the pier."

"Sounds amazing." I sighed. He squeezed my hand once more and strolled toward the door. "Isaac?"

"Yes?" He asked, turning to face me.

"Don't wait so long to call next time."

"I promise. You don't have to worry about that anymore."

17
PLANS

"Gwyn, I figured out how to get you to Veronica's reception without your aunt finding out," Denise said as I closed my bedroom door behind us.

"You're always scheming, aren't you?" I teased. "So, what's the plan?"

I plopped down on my bed and tossed Denise the latest issue of *Seventeen*. She sat down on the floor and opened the Ziploc bag of homemade chocolate chip cookies we had swiped from the kitchen counter.

"Okay, so you are going to help me paint my room on Sunday, right?"

"Yes, that's right." I nodded.

"What if you told your aunt you were planning to spend Saturday night with me? You could get to my house at about four, change for the reception, and then come back to my house when the party's over." Denise smiled, obviously pleased with herself for coming up with such a good idea.

"That might work, Denise. You could go ahead and take my dress to your house. That way, Aunt Delia won't accidentally find it. The dress is still in my trunk."

"No problem. And that would give me the opportunity to help you with the makeup and hair situation."

"What makeup and hair situation?" I said sharply.

"Oh, come on, Gwyn. You know you need some help. The only updo you can manage is a ponytail."

"I guess you're right about the hair, but my makeup is fine."

Denise rolled her eyes. I threw a pillow at her, and she deftly moved to the left so the pillow hit the closet door instead of her head. The noise must have startled Cher from her nap because she hissed and leapt to attack the pillow.

"Okay, back to the task at hand—your makeup. Here, look at this picture." Denise folded the magazine and pointed to a Cover-Girl advertisement. "See, she's not wearing those gaudy colors."

"Gaudy?" I pursed my lips and gave Denise a sideways glance.

"Blue eyeliner doesn't go with everything, Gwyn."

"I don't wear blue all the time."

"Okay, so sometimes silver or grass green." Denise rolled her eyes again.

I aimed another pillow at Denise and, this time, I met my target.

"Fine, Gwyn, I'll stop. Let's talk about something else." Denise closed the magazine and set it aside. She pulled a cookie from the bag. "I want to hear about Isaac. Have you talked to him lately?"

"Well, actually, he came by work today."

"He did?" Denise eagerly moved towards the bed, kneeled on the floor, and propped her elbows in front of me. "Don't make me wait! What did he say?"

"Well, he's planning something for my birthday. He wants me to meet him at the pier after work next Wednesday, then he's going to eat dinner with us at Sal's."

"I'm sure your mom will love Isaac."

"I hope so, because I really like him, Denise. I've never liked anyone this much."

"I'm really happy for you. You deserve this." Denise smiled and handed me the bag of cookies. "So, has he kissed you yet?"

"Not that again." I covered my face with my hand and shook my head. "No, Denise, no."

Almost as if on cue, Aunt Delia knocked while opening the door to my bedroom. Her knock was never a request for entrance, but rather more like an announcement.

"Gwyn, Denise, I hope you are having a good time."

"Hi, Aunt Delia. Yes, we are."

"Hello, Mrs. James," Denise said politely.

"Now, Denise, you will stay for dinner, won't you? Mr. James is out of town, and I cannot get used to cooking for three."

"I'm sure that will be fine. I'll give my mom a call to let her know. Thank you."

"And you will be here for Gwyn's birthday luncheon on Thursday, correct?"

"Yes, ma'am, I wouldn't miss it." Denise turned and winked at me. I returned a relieved smile.

"Gwyn, I wanted to give you an early birthday present."

"Oh, thanks, but you could have waited until tomorrow." My eyes widened with surprise. I could not remember when my aunt breached protocol and gave a gift early.

"Don't worry, Gwyn, I still saved one for your special day," my aunt said with an uncharacteristic joy in her voice.

Denise and I shared a startled glance. Aunt Delia was being unusually friendly, which unnerved me.

"I bought you a lovely outfit to wear to the luncheon," Aunt Delia said.

She pulled out the clothing that she had been hiding behind her back. She held up one coat hanger displaying a pale-yellow cardigan set in one hand, and a knee-length floral pencil skirt in the other. She beamed with a genuine smile.

"That's really nice, Mrs. James. Isn't it, Gwyn?" Denise eyed me in an annoying mother-like fashion.

"Um, yeah." I scratched my head. "Don't get me wrong, Aunt Delia, it's a really nice outfit, but it's not exactly me." I scoured my mind for some excuse not to wear it.

"I know. I thought a change would be nice. Mrs. Jenkins will be there, as well as my cousin, and Carrie. You want to look nice, don't you?"

"Yes, ma'am, but—" I gathered my thoughts. "But I don't have shoes." Aunt Delia hung the two coat hangers on the doorknob and picked up a shoebox that she had placed in the hallway. She lifted out a pair of white sandals that matched the background of the skirt. "No excuses." She grinned.

At eleven years old, all I wanted was to blend in with the crowd. If I wore the same clothing and participated in the same activities as everyone else, I could exist unnoticed, but my aunt would have none of that. When I wanted to take piano lessons like all the other girls in my class, she registered me for French horn, and when my friends wore argyle sweaters and corduroys, she had me in expensive Laura Ashley dresses with puff-sleeves. Now at eighteen, when I longed to stand out from the crowd, she tried to mold me into every other *proper young lady*, the type who would become a bank teller or real estate agent.

Aunt Delia returned the shoes to their box and placed it on my dresser. "Okay, girls. Dinner should be ready in about thirty minutes. Denise, don't forget to call your mom."

"I won't," she said before my aunt turned and bounded down the stairs. We waited until we heard her heels cross the hardwood floor at the base of the stairs before we spoke.

"Denise, I can't wear that. I'll look ridiculous."

"It's only your friends, Gwyn," she said, obviously trying her best to console me. "No one will think less of you. You can't fight the system every day."

Denise playfully tilted her head and smirked.

"Maybe to spare an argument, I'll have to suck it up," I conceded.

"Yeah, but no one said you couldn't accessorize." Denise smiled and tossed me a black plastic bangle that laid on my desk.

I caught the bangle and slipped it on my wrist. I held out my arm and spun the bracelet. "Now, if I only had a yellow one."

18
ADULTHOOD

For my sixteenth birthday, Mom fought for me to get my own phone line. At first, Aunt Delia opposed it, something about the impropriety of staying up all night talking to boys. I don't know what my mom said to finally convince her why I needed one, and I never asked.

The night before my eighteenth birthday was the first time I had ever stayed up all night talking to a boy. After about six hours, I fell asleep with the receiver buried in my pillow. I don't believe Isaac and I said a word for the last hour, but neither one wanted to be the first to hang up. When I awoke three hours later to the sound of my alarm, I found Cher poised to attack the phone as an incessant beep warned the receiver was off the hook. I slowly rose from bed, picked up the phone, and returned it to my desk.

For the past three years, Mrs. Jenkins only scheduled me for a half-day on my birthday but today, four hours still seemed like a lifetime. Isaac had asked me to meet him at the pier after work, so I planned to consume a large amount of caffeine beforehand. I refused to allow fatigue to destroy one moment of what he might have planned.

I had forgotten to remove my contacts before the marathon call, so bloodshot eyes stared back at me from the bathroom mirror. A circular indentation encompassed my left cheekbone, because the receiver pressed into my face for the better part of the night. After I splashed my face with cold water, I examined my reflection and grinned.

Whatever. It was my eighteenth birthday, and I had Isaac.

After showering and drinking a cup of Aunt Delia's strong coffee, I felt better prepared to face the morning. I slipped on my black cotton miniskirt and the white T-shirt with Audrey Hepburn screen printed on the front, an early present from Mom.

When I arrived at the store, Mrs. Jenkins greeted me enthusiastically and moved away from the counter to reveal a huge bouquet of white roses and blue hydrangeas.

"Oh, Mrs. Jenkins, it's beautiful." Mrs. Jenkins surprised me with something for my birthday every year. Last year, she gave me this cool arrangement of succulents, but I didn't have the heart to tell her that I killed them by placing the container too close to the air conditioning vent. At least a bouquet wasn't supposed to last more than a week.

Mrs. Jenkins gave me a hug. "I'm so glad. I wanted to do something special for your birthday. You do so much around here, and I love you for it."

"Thank you so much." I picked up the tan teddy bear that sat in front of the vase and rubbed his cute little ears. "You didn't have to do this."

"Now stop it; I wanted to. Besides, I know your aunt has a luncheon planned for you tomorrow, and this will make the perfect centerpiece."

"I agree." I smiled at her. "Are you coming? My aunt said she sent you an invitation."

"Yes, I'll be there. I am going to close the shop for an extra lunch hour. The customers will just have to wait." Mrs. Jenkins dug in the pocket of her smock for her keys. "I am going to make the deliveries and be back before you leave today. I'll take your flowers to the house, so you won't have to carry them."

"Thanks. They are wonderful."

"And so are you, dear." Mrs. Jenkins lifted the vase carefully, and I held the door open for her. "Hold down the fort while I'm gone. Bye, now."

I had thought the anticipation of my afternoon with Isaac would make the day agonizingly long but to my surprise, the four hours passed quickly.

I pulled into the small dirt parking lot adjacent to the pier and parked next to Isaac's 1980s Volvo. The boardwalk leading to the river led me to Isaac kneeling on a picnic blanket under the pergola. I paused for a moment, watching him push candles into decorated cupcakes. I wanted to freeze the moment in my memory.

I moved a few steps forward as he lifted his head to look at me.

Isaac grinned. "You made it. Happy birthday."

I opened my mouth, but no sound escaped. I was at a loss for words. After an awkward silence, in lieu of speaking, I ran and hugged him. My head fit perfectly in the space under his chin.

"Thank you," I whispered.

"You're very welcome." He moved my shoulders back with his hands so he could look at me.

I didn't know if I should speak or smile. I stood as a foreigner in my own body.

"You're beautiful, do you know that?" Isaac said.

I glanced down at my Converse sneakers and back up to meet his eyes.

"No one's really told me that before, except my mom, but I don't think that counts."

"Well, I think so, and that should count." He smiled and softly cupped my cheek in his hand.

"It does," I whispered.

And then it happened.

He brought my face toward his and kissed me. I closed my eyes and let the world fall away. I no longer sensed the wooden planks beneath me and the intense July heat. All I could feel were his lips against mine.

As he slowly pulled away, his breath brushed my face.

"Happy birthday," he said softly.

"I think you already said that," I teased.

"I probably did." Isaac audibly exhaled. "My mind is swirling. I can't think straight."

"It's a good feeling, isn't it?"

He nodded. We stood in silence, with our arms around each other. I heard the movement of the swamp grass and the rustle of a heron taking flight. The bird cast a shadow over us for a fleeting second as it flew overhead.

"I have something for you." He released me and bent down to pick up a package wrapped with blue striped paper. "Sorry, I couldn't find any birthday paper."

"That's okay. You didn't have to get me anything."

"I wanted to. Here, open it."

I tore back the paper to reveal the word *Boston*.

"It's a guidebook," Isaac said enthusiastically. "Full color, with transit maps and everything."

"It's perfect, thank you." I flipped through the glossy pages. "This is the most thoughtful gift, Isaac."

"I'm glad you like it. I wrote a list of all the museums and restaurants I want to see with you when I visit. Here, it's in the front." He pulled out a piece of paper from behind the book's cover. "We can check them off as we go. You'll only be a train ride away from me."

"Is that so?" I smiled.

"Only a little seven-hour trip on the Northeast Regional." As I held the guidebook, Isaac flipped to the section titled "Getting There," pointing to the Amtrak route.

"You have this all figured out, don't you?"

"I do." He grinned with his eyes fixed on mine. I desperately tried not to blink so I wouldn't miss a fraction of this moment.

I clutched the book against my chest with one hand and ran my fingers through his hair with the other. I lightly kissed him. "Thank you."

He rested his forehead against mine. My awareness of the July heat suddenly rushed back, as beads of sweat formed on my skin.

"You know we should probably eat these cupcakes before the icing melts," I said.

I sat down in the shade underneath the pergola as he lit the candles on the four oversized cupcakes with bright blue icing.

"Okay now, blow them out and make a wish."

I closed my eyes and blew my hopes into the thick summer air.

ISAAC and I arrived at the restaurant to be greeted by my mom and Charlie, the on-again, off-again boyfriend, in the parking lot. My heart sank a little when I saw Charlie. It's not that I didn't like him —I did. I guess I had imagined Dad standing there instead, even though I knew my mom would never have invited him. That was something my Uncle Beckett would do.

In the past week, Mom and Charlie had reunited, but I couldn't discern how long the relationship would last this time. I was ecstatic to have a break from Alanis Morissette's *Jagged Little Pill* album, which had become Mom's go-to break-up album, being played on a loop.

Mom pressed her cheek to mine. "How's my baby girl?"

"Good," I said.

"I hope you don't mind, Charlie really wanted to come celebrate your birthday," she said.

"That's fine." I turned to Charlie, who stood next to Mom with an uncomfortable grin, holding the ribbons attached to three helium balloons. One read *Happy 18th Birthday* in red. "Thanks for coming. It's really nice of you."

"You're welcome, kiddo."

Charlie began calling me *kiddo* when I met him five years ago. I think it was the only term of endearment he knew for a child.

"I thought you would like these," he said. "Everybody needs birthday balloons." He handed me the balloon bouquet. My mom squeezed his elbow and turned to smile at him.

"Thanks." I studied the colorful ribbons, which were tied to a star-shaped weight. I traced the edge of the star with my finger. My dad gave me birthday balloons every year but in order to get them into the house, I would lie to Aunt Delia and tell her they were from my uncle. Uncle Beckett would always play along, since he was the one who invited my dad to Sal's in the first place. I wondered if my uncle called Dad this year to tell him why he couldn't come. Isaac touched my shoulder which brought my thoughts back to the present.

"Oh, Mom, Charlie—this is Isaac."

"It's really nice to meet you." Mom started to reach out to shake his hand, but she seemed to decide at the last moment to hug him instead. "I couldn't be happier."

"It's nice to meet you, too, Ms. Madison."

"Oh, please call me Trisha. I may be Gwyn's mom, but I'm not old enough to be a missus yet." She winked at me.

"Okay." Isaac paused, then said, "Trisha."

"And I'm glad to meet you as well." Charlie reached out to shake Isaac's hand.

"Me too. It's nice to finally meet Gwyn's family."

"Danny and Denise are waiting for us inside," Mom said. "We tried to get Crystal to wait on us, but Sal Junior insisted."

"Wonderful." I rolled my eyes before turning to Isaac. "Well, let's face the inevitable. Sal Junior is an experience in itself."

Charlie held the restaurant door as Isaac and I followed Mom inside. Danny and Denise were sitting at a long table toward the back of the main dining room. They waved vigorously.

As we proceeded toward the table, I surveyed the room to make sure I did not see anyone I recognized, or more importantly, anyone my aunt associated with.

Our table was partially hidden from the main dining room by a wooden partition, which stopped about four feet from the ceiling. Terra-cotta pots of ivy filled the gap between the top of the partition and the ceiling. Thankfully, the chairs designated for Isaac and me were behind the safety of the greenery.

I sat at the head of the table in a chair adorned with streamers. Isaac sat to my right, next to Denise, and across from my mom. Of course, Charlie sat next to Mom. I assumed my mom planned the seating arrangement so she could get a good look at her daughter's boyfriend. The vacant seat directly across from me, at the far end of the table, left me feeling exposed. I almost expected Uncle Beckett to walk through the door and take his seat, but I knew that was wishful thinking.

Mom poured soda into our glasses from a red translucent pitcher. "We already ordered the pizzas, Gwyn. Breadsticks are coming too. I asked for extra marinara because I know how much you love it. Oh, I am so glad you all are here!"

Mom squeezed Charlie's forearm and then clasped her hands together. Charlie grinned and shook his head. She had a habit of talking excessively when she was excited. "You'll have to tell me everything that's going on. I miss being a young adult; so many exciting things happen. Danny, Denise tells me you got a new car for graduation. Do you love it?"

"Yes, ma'am, I—" Danny began.

"I know you do, and I'm sure your mom is happy you guys are staying around next year," my mom interjected. "There are so many opportunities right here."

I caught my breath at my mom's words. Isaac must have noticed, because he lightly squeezed my knee underneath the table, then laid his hand on mine, as my hand clutched the edge of my chair. I knew my mom was just making conversation, but every word hit me like a dagger.

Charlie put his arm around my mom, as if to encourage her to stop talking. Suddenly realizing the significance of her words, she blushed. I mouthed, "It's okay."

"Um, yes, I am sure she is," Danny said. "But Denise and I are planning to transfer to a school out west in a couple years."

Danny openly admitted that he played around in high school. He maintained a C average, but somehow managed a four and five on his AP Calculus and AP Biology exams, respectively.

It's hard enough to be a nerdy girl in this small town, but for the guys, I think it was ten times worse. I never felt the expectation to party and screw around, but I knew the guys experienced that pressure regularly. I heard them talk. Every Monday counting up how many drinks they had and with whom, like they were gathering research data. Danny would have gotten into much more trouble if Denise wasn't in his life. He might have enjoyed a party, but he took commitments and loyalty seriously.

"And you two." Denise pointed to Isaac and me. "Y'all better come visit us."

"Hopefully, she'll keep me around that long," Isaac said.

"I have a feeling she will," Denise said with a wink in my direction.

"So how did you two meet anyway?" Charlie asked, leaning forward. At least for now, the story of how Isaac and I met would be embellished with a few white lies.

"Well—" Isaac cleared his throat. "Gwyn delivered flowers to my mom that I had ordered. To be honest, I was a little rude when we first met. What can I say? She woke me up when she rang the doorbell." Isaac absentmindedly ran his hand through his thick hair. "I don't think I said more than two words to her."

"Come to think of it, you were a little rude." I nudged him. "Your mom even agreed."

"Okay, stop, so we've established that I'm rude," Isaac said playfully. "Now would you let me finish this story?" He winked at me, and I nodded for him to continue.

My mother tilted her head towards me. I heard her quietly giggle.

"I knew where she worked, so I decided to visit her the next day. I don't know, something compelled me to go. I even thought of bringing bagels as a peace offering."

Isaac presented the story with such conviction. The expressions on Mom and Charlie's faces told me they bought the entire story—hook, line, and sinker. Denise and Danny were folding creations with their straw wrappers. By now they had heard both the true and imagined stories of our meeting, and I knew they could care less about hearing either again.

"What woman can say no to bagels?" Charlie rubbed my mom's shoulder. "And then, I suppose, the rest is history."

"I guess you could say so. It wasn't something I expected to happen this summer, but I'm glad it did." Isaac leaned toward me and attempted to put his arm around my shoulder, but Mom's pre-arranged seating configuration made the move awkward, so he settled for kissing me on my right temple.

I had hung on Isaac's every word. A part of me wanted to be embarrassed. I hated being the center of attention, but another part of me relished every moment. Denise sighed, and everyone fell silent, allowing the sound of the ceiling fan above our table to grow louder.

Sal Junior, balancing three pizzas, interrupted the stillness.

"I heard it was my favorite customer's birthday!" Sal Junior placed the pizzas on the silver pedestals positioned in the middle of the table. He wore a red V-neck T-shirt that exposed black chest hair accentuated by a gold necklace. He slipped behind Mom and Charlie's chairs, wrapped his arm roughly around my neck, and kissed me on the cheek. It happened so quickly that I did not have time to protest.

Isaac coughed, and Sal Junior shot him a look.

"Who's this guy, Gwyn?" Sal Junior asked.

"Um, well—" I said, searching for the right words.

"The boyfriend." Isaac jutted out his hand to shake Sal Junior's, which Sal took reluctantly. Mom and Denise, no longer able to contain their laughter, both snorted. Isaac attempted to maintain a serious expression.

Sal Junior stepped back. "How long has this been going on?"

"I guess about three weeks," I said. "But Sal, you know we, you and me, would never work."

I couldn't believe what I was saying, but with the pitiful look in Sal Junior's eyes, I knew I had to let him down easy.

"Yeah, you're probably right." He leaned close to me and whispered, "Now if he hurts you, you know who to call."

"You'll be the first one, Sal." I patted Sal Junior's shoulder as if he was a small child.

Isaac set down his empty glass with an audible thud, signaling Sal to leave.

"Oh, you need more soda. I'll be back." Sal Junior picked up the pitcher and hurried away.

"Wow, he's a character," Isaac said.

Denise swirled a breadstick in her bowl of marinara. "You've got nothing to worry about. He might look brawny, but I assure you, he's harmless."

"Okay, time for gifts." Danny handed me a present wrapped in *Peanuts* comics.

"Danny, you didn't have to get me anything. We normally don't exchange birthday gifts."

"This one I just couldn't resist," he said slyly.

A small robot keychain dangled from the ribbon. One look at the little toy's red beady eyes and I could guess what was in the package. I didn't know whether to laugh or throw something at him.

"If you press the robot's stomach, his eyes light up like a flashlight." Danny stood up and leaned across the table to demonstrate.

"Wow, that's cool." Isaac took the keychain and traced circles of light on the ceiling.

I tore away the paper to reveal the cover of *I, Robot*. The very same edition Uncle Beckett encouraged him to buy.

"Science fiction? I didn't know you liked that stuff, Gwyn." Mom picked up the book and ran her fingers over the embossed cover before handing it to Isaac, who practically jumped with excitement.

"Oh, she loves this one, Ms. Trisha," Denise responded with laughter in her eyes.

Isaac examined the end sheets closely. "It's awesome. Do you know how rare this edition is?"

"Yeah, well, you know, I do love a good classic," Danny said, leaning back in his chair and crossing his arms.

I rolled my eyes and threw a breadstick at him.

"What was that for?" Danny glared at me.

"Just be glad it wasn't covered with tomato sauce, buddy," I said with a smirk.

"Okay, my turn." Denise handed me a bright pink envelope. When I opened the enclosed birthday card, a gift certificate for Salon West fell into my lap.

"What's this, Denise?"

"Well, since your aunt was forcing you to wear that Sunday School outfit tomorrow, you could at least have great hair. Since you're off, I thought it would work out perfectly." Denise clasped her hands in delight and her eyes brightened with excitement. "You have an appointment tomorrow morning at nine. I'm going to pick you up at eight-thirty."

"That is so nice. I don't know what to say. You're gonna have to help me figure out what to do with this." I ran my hands through my mass of curly hair.

"Don't worry, I think your mom and I can handle that," Denise said. "Right, Ms. Trisha?"

"Oh yeah, I've been waiting for this. I started cutting pictures out of *Glamour* ever since Denise told me."

"Mom, I don't look that bad, do I?"

"No, honey, just a little raw. A diamond in the rough."

"*Mother*," I said, over-emphasizing the last syllable.

Isaac grabbed my hand. "Well, I think she is beautiful just the way she is."

"Of course, you do, sweetheart," Mom addressed Isaac, before turning to me. "We all do. But a little updating never hurt anyone."

"Trisha, why don't we give her our gift?" Charlie pushed back the chair next to him and reached under the table to pull out a very large box. "Come over here, Gwyn, and open it."

I sighed with relief, thankful that Charlie was always able to read a room well. You could count on him to divert the conversation when things got uncomfortable—especially when Mom needed diverting.

I slipped out of my seat and stood next to Charlie as he set the box on the table. I ripped off the wrapping paper to reveal the words "Sony," "CD changer," and "Hi-Fi Sound System."

"A stereo? That's amazing! Thanks, Mom, Charlie."

"You're welcome." Mom broke out into a wide grin. "It's for your dorm room. I know how you like to listen to music when you write papers."

"I'm going to carve your name on the bottom, so no one will steal it," Charlie said seriously.

"Sorta like when Aunt Delia wrote my name in all of my clothes before I went to summer camp." I patted Charlie on the back and smiled at him. "Thanks, that's really sweet of you."

"No problem, kiddo."

"That's a terrific stereo, Gwyn," Crystal said as she set a filled pitcher of soda on the table.

"Thanks—um, what happened to Sal Junior?" I asked with confusion.

"I don't know, he asked me to bring this over." Crystal shrugged, her red hair swaying with her shoulders. "Okay then, enjoy your birthday. Nice to see you all."

"You, too, Crystal," Denise said.

"Gwyn, there's one more present," Denise said. "Beckett had called your dad to say he would be out of town for your birthday, so your dad mailed your present to me."

Denise handed me a finely wrapped box embellished with a

purple ribbon. A gold label with the address of a jewelry store was affixed to the top. I couldn't remember my dad ever giving me jewelry. He was more of a stuffed animal kind of guy. I opened the box and pulled out a silver-linked bracelet with a bauble of black onyx surrounded by silver filigree.

Eager to get a closer look, Denise walked around the table and looked over my shoulder. "That's beautiful. He has really great taste."

"He always did," Mom said quietly.

I rubbed the black stone between my fingers and flipped it over to find an engraving. *Love always, Dad. 7.16.1998.* I glanced at the stereo sitting in front of the vacant chair.

I missed him. I missed my dad.

Isaac studied me with tenderness in his eyes. He smiled as I wiped away an escaping tear.

After the birthday cake and two more awkward interactions with Sal Junior, we finally left the restaurant. Charlie helped carry the stereo to my car, and we pushed the balloons into the back seat.

Denise hugged me. "I'll see you in the morning. Get ready to shock your aunt."

I squeezed her back. "I can't wait."

"We're headed out too." Charlie placed his arm around my mom.

"I'll see you at home, babe," she said and blew me a kiss.

"Okay, Mom. Love you."

"Love you too."

Soon, Isaac and I found ourselves alone in the restaurant parking lot, standing between our cars, which were parked next to one another. Isaac leaned against the passenger door of his Volvo. I took a step toward him. He reached out for my waist and pulled me close to him.

"You're a lot more suave than you think you are," I teased.

"Oh, am I?" he asked.

"You're the one who said you were awkward around girls."

"I can trip on something if that would make you feel better."

"No need for that." I rested my hand on his shoulder. "Thanks for coming to my birthday party."

"I wanted to." Isaac reached up and tucked my hair behind my ear and rested his forehead against mine. He kissed the space between my eyes, and then his lips traveled down my cheek to meet mine.

I closed my eyes, attempting to block out racing thoughts. I tried to concentrate on Isaac, and me, and this moment, but thoughts of my family and the secrecy that seemed to cover every inch of my life, could not be calmed. Isaac drew me closer, and I rested my cheek against his chest.

"It must have been hard growing up without your dad."

"Yeah, but my uncle did his best to make up for it." I opened my eyes. Through the windows of the Volvo, I observed a seagull push the gravel in the parking lot with his beak. We were only about three blocks from the river, but the bird still seemed out of place against the backdrop of crushed granite.

"I know your uncle must adore you."

With my head still nuzzled against his chest, I smiled as a second seagull landed beside the first. He didn't look so lonely anymore.

"He calls me his Gwynnie."

"Well, I can't wait to meet him."

"He'll love you, especially your taste in books."

"Yeah, what was all that about anyway? It had to be big—you wasted a breadstick and all."

I lightly pinched Isaac's side. He let out a small yelp and playfully pinned my arm against him.

"Okay, tell me, Gwyn."

"Fine, let's just say, I would never have met you if it wasn't for that book."

"I guess that's good enough." He lifted my head and put his hands on my shoulders so I could look him in the eyes. "So, you aren't going to tell me the story, huh?"

"Sorry, some other time," I said coyly. Suddenly the pair of seagulls jumped to flight as the sound of a heavy car pushing through gravel grew louder.

"Get down," I whispered frantically, pushing Isaac into a squat beside the car.

A spray of rocks jumped a few feet ahead of us as Isaac lost his footing and landed on his bottom. "What was that for?"

"Ruthie McCall." I said, taking deep, sharp breaths. "She pulled in front of the restaurant. I would recognize her green Buick anywhere."

"Who's Ruthie McCall?"

"Our neighbor—our nosy neighbor, I should add. I don't want Aunt Delia to find out about us from her."

Hidden behind the protection of Isaac's car, we waited until old Ruthie left the restaurant with her takeout order. After the green Buick disappeared from the parking lot, the seagulls returned to scavenge for little crumbs the car churned up in its wake.

19
SKINNY-DIPPING

My mother had hung the full-length mirror on my closet door according to her height, so I always saw my headless reflection, and today, I looked like a headless third-grade Sunday school teacher. My eyes moved from the white patent-leather sandals to the knee-length floral skirt, to the faux-pearl buttons on the yellow cardigan. I had emerged as my aunt's own version of herself at eighteen—that is, from the neck down.

I lowered into a squat in front of the mirror to admire my new haircut. The pencil skirt hugged me more than expected, which constrained my ability to bend down fully. Aunt Delia obviously perceived me as the build of my mother. I contorted my head to the side to see myself. Denise had brought a folder to the salon filled with magazine headshots of celebrities. Under Denise's direction, my hair had been layered and cut to frame my face, my curls perfectly defined.

I turned to the left to study the perfect, professionally rendered fuchsia stripe that began at the crown of my head and ended in a curl at my shoulder. I smiled at the thought of Aunt Delia's face when she saw my hair, but then my racing heart reminded me of the fear her eyes could induce. The fuchsia stripe matched the flowers in the skirt, and Aunt Delia liked a coordinated outfit.

I wanted to be seen as rebellious, not defiant—like an intellectually rebellious person who rallied against conformity and fought the constraints of tradition. Although, in reality, I was a chicken. I might as well cluck my way downstairs, flapping my arms to distract the awaiting wolf from the fuchsia stripe.

My cousin, Carrie, and her mom, Georgia, had already arrived. I stood at the top of the staircase, taking in the noise from below. Georgia and my mom were engaged in a lively conversation in the living room, the sound of which rose above dishes clanging in the kitchen.

"Hey, aren't you coming down?" Carrie asked, looking up at me from the foot of the stairs.

"I think I'm immobile." I stared at my feet.

"Don't be a goof. Come down here." She gestured me forward.

I had always been envious of Carrie's self-confidence. She spoke her mind, and no one ever seemed to condemn her for it. Maybe that was a perk of being beautiful. I slowly navigated each step. The strap of my wedge sandals slipped off my heels as I walked.

Carrie bounced my curls in the palm of her hand. "Your hair is amazing. Has your mom seen it?"

"Not yet."

"She's going to love it." Carrie sashayed in a circle around me, admiring my new look.

"Are you that confident about Aunt Delia's reaction too?" I asked.

"Hmm, well..." She tilted her head.

"See, even you aren't sure."

"You know what I think?" Carrie propped her hand on her waist. "On the outside, Aunt Delia may appear prudish, but on the inside, I think she likes that you're a little rebellious."

"What makes you say that?"

"Just some stuff my mom said she and Aunt Delia used to do as kids."

Aunt Delia didn't talk much about her childhood, but Georgia, six months older than my aunt, was happy to fill in juicy details.

"Okay, like what?" I asked eagerly.

"Oh, I don't know; something about skinny-dipping." Carrie clasped her hands with excitement. "They did it on a dare, and each won ten dollars in return."

My eyes bulged.

"Apparently," Carrie continued, "Aunt Delia wasn't always the serious woman that she is now."

"When did you find this out?"

"My mom showed me an old photo album. There were a bunch of pictures with Delia and her friend LuLu. Fully clothed, don't worry. Apparently, LuLu and Delia were a wild pair."

"Wow." I scrunched my forehead. "What do you think changed her?"

Before Carrie could respond, I answered my own question. *Adam*.

"Who knows? We all have a past I guess," Carrie said, shrugging her shoulders.

"Yeah, I suppose that's true."

"You know, she also talks about all your art awards."

"Really?" I asked.

Carrie nodded. My brow furrowed in surprise. Aunt Delia never did much more than hang my awards on the refrigerator.

"Well. I'm glad you're here. I don't think I could survive one of these birthday luncheons without you."

I hugged my cousin tightly around the neck. Her diamond stud earring pressed into my cheek, which hurt enough to make me wince.

"Don't worry, I'll figure out a way for you to pay me back." Carrie grinned and looked me up and down. "Something that involves you wearing that outfit again."

"Now you're scaring me."

"Come on," she said, linking her arm in mine. "We don't want to keep your guests waiting."

I rolled my eyes and allowed my cousin to pull me into the dining room. The flower arrangement from Mrs. Jenkins was positioned in the middle of the table with Aunt Delia's fine china expertly placed around it. The blue linen napkins matched the hydrangeas that spilled over the rim of the clear glass vase. A place card, decorated with a name in perfect handwriting, sat above each place setting. Next to each place card, she positioned a white votive tied with a blue ribbon. My mom, Denise, and Mrs. Jenkins stood behind their chairs.

Cousin Georgia carried in a bowl of fruit salad from the kitchen.

"There's the birthday girl." She balanced the bowl in the crook of her arm and pulled the door closed behind her. "Let me set this down and give you a hug."

Mom took the bowl from Georgia and set it on the table.

"How long has it been, sweetheart?" Georgia asked, kissing my cheek.

"Since Christmas, I think. Thanks for coming." I smiled at her.

Cousin Georgia did not mention the bright pink stripe that was nose distance away from her as she hugged me, but then again, she wasn't known for being observant.

"You're very welcome." She hugged me again. "Come to the table you two. Delia will be right in with the iced tea."

Carrie and I took our places behind our chairs.

"Looks like you've been busy since I saw you yesterday," Mrs. Jenkins said with a hint of sarcasm.

"Oh, yeah, I guess so," I replied, not sure of what she was referring to.

"Isn't it great?" Denise chimed in with excitement. "I took her to the salon this morning."

"Your hair looks good. It fits you." Mrs. Jenkins winked at me.

Cousin Georgia placed a butter knife on the table. "Funny. You'd think I'd notice a pink stripe."

"Gwyn would need a Mohawk for you to notice," Mom responded. Cousin Georgia pretended to throw a roll at her from across the table.

Mom pointed to the kitchen door. "You better watch it, Georgia, or my sister will have you scrubbing the floors." Mom's laughter fired in short snorting bursts, as she tried not to erupt.

The accordion door to the kitchen screeched open. Aunt Delia carried a glass pitcher in one hand and a silver trivet in the other. She set the trivet carefully on the table followed by the pitcher. "Are we ready to eat, ladies?"

My aunt pulled out her chair to sit down, and we did the same. Aunt Delia's eyes moved in an arch from the left side of my head to the right without blinking.

After several awkward seconds, Aunt Delia finally spoke. "Happy Birthday, Gwyn. I'm glad the skirt fits you well." She picked up the basket of rolls and placed one on her bread plate before handing the basket to Mrs. Jenkins.

"Thank you, Aunt Delia," I said.

I swallowed hard. I had been holding my breath, waiting for an onslaught of criticism, but remarkably, none came. Lunch passed without so much as a comment about my hair or a discussion of my college plans. The conversation centered around Carrie's upcoming semester abroad in Spain, Mrs. Jenkins's plans for a store expansion, Mom's rekindled love for Charlie, and Denise's new car. I don't believe anyone noticed that Aunt Delia and I hardly spoke during lunch. Neither my aunt nor I had patience for small talk.

Another trait we apparently shared.

"HONEY, pay no attention to what those girls say." Aunt Delia sat down next to me on the brick steps of the front porch. I was ten years old.

I held my knees close to my body and stared at the flagstones leading to the driveway.

"I hate them, Auntie," I mumbled through my tears. "They are so mean."

"That's the way insecure girls are. Enduring their remarks will only make you stronger, Gwyn."

"Why can't God find an easier way to make me stronger?" I asked, hugging my knees closer.

Aunt Delia chuckled and patted my back.

"It will get better, I promise," she said with assurance. "You know we're alike, you and me."

I looked up at her. My tears left a sticky trail on my cheeks. "How do you figure that?" I asked quietly.

"We both have smarts." She touched my knee and smiled. "Mark my words, Gwyn. One day, all those pretty girls will be answering to us."

That day, Aunt Delia's chestnut brown hair was not fixed in its usual bun but instead fell in soft waves below her shoulders, in preparation for Uncle Beckett's college alumni event. Her fitted blue dress showed off her thin waist and bright eyes. Aunt Delia always seemed to behave as if she wasn't good enough for Uncle Beck's college friends, because the handful of times they got together, she would dress completely out of character.

"You're pretty, Aunt Delia. I've always thought so." I wiped my nose with the back of my hand.

She tugged a stem on the rose bush that grew next to our front door. She broke off a flower, making sure the remaining stem had no thorns, and handed it to me. I twirled the stem between my fingers. My eyes followed her as she entered the kitchen, and the screen door bounced shut behind her.

I DID NOT NOTICE Aunt Delia excuse herself from the table until she appeared by my side, holding an unopened package with the words *Happy Birthday* written in Uncle Beckett's slanted script across one side of the brown box.

"What's this, Aunt Delia?" I asked.

"It arrived from your uncle a couple days ago. I thought you might enjoy opening it today," she said cheerfully, placing the package in front of me.

I tugged on the clear packaging tape and pulled it loose from the cardboard flaps.

"Hurry up, Gwyn, we want to see," said Denise, who always tore into presents as if the universe owed them to her.

"Just wait a second." I removed wads of white tissue paper.

Aunt Delia picked up the discarded paper I had tossed on the table and stuffed it in the pocket of her apron. I paused and ran my finger across the edge of a mahogany jewelry box that had been hidden by the tissue. The lid was inset with a stained-glass butterfly.

Mrs. Jenkins leaned across the table for a better look. "Isn't that beautiful."

"What's inside?" Mom asked. "Open up the box. Let's see."

I opened the lid. A plain, cream-colored card laid in the box with the words *For my Gwynnie on her eighteenth birthday* written inside. I lifted the card to see what hid underneath. I drew an audible breath. The diamond and sapphire engagement ring stared back at me. Catherine's ring. I heard Aunt Delia gasp. I dared not turn around. I could not face her.

Carrie slid her chair closer to mine. "What is it, Gwyn? It must be good from that reaction." She reached over me, picked up the ring, and held it up to the light of the chandelier. "God, that's gorgeous. And it's real too."

Denise gestured for Carrie to pass her the ring. "I want a rich uncle, but I have to settle for one that's wanted in four states for writing bad checks." Denise slid the ring on her finger and examined it from an arm's distance.

"Denise, you are too much." Mom turned to me. "I bet that ring was in Nana Lola's family. What do you think?"

"Could be," I said, attempting to sound underwhelmed. "I guess I am the only child in Uncle's family to hand the ring down to." The lump in my throat grew larger.

"That's true, but regardless, it's such a sweet gift. He probably saved it all these years for your eighteenth birthday," Mom said. "Go ahead, try it on."

I slipped the ring on my right hand and spread my fingers. Catherine was the last person to wear this ring. I started to tremble —but hopefully not enough for anyone to notice.

I turned toward the sound of crumpling paper. Aunt Delia's hand clenched inside the pocket of her apron, her knuckles moving underneath the fabric.

"Delia, are you okay?" Cousin Georgia asked, rising from her chair. She moved toward my aunt and gripped her by the elbow. "You look flushed. Here, sit down."

Aunt Delia waved her off. "No, no, I'm fine, Georgia. Just a bit light-headed from the heat in the kitchen."

I knew she was lying. I recognized the panic in her eyes, because the same was in mine. The panic that came before secrets erupted.

20
FRENZY

*A*fter the luncheon, I packed my duffel bag to take to Denise's. Truthfully, it was Denise who packed my bag as I watched. While rifling through my bathroom drawers looking for makeup and bobby pins, Denise talked excitedly about my secret date with Isaac punctuated with stray thoughts about her new room décor. I hoped the mundane task of painting her bedroom would distract me from the chaos I had created. Once I became a liar, it was hard to stop.

I SPENT Saturday morning running errands. I needed a few last-minute essentials, primarily deodorant and a razor. After pulling into our driveway, a queasiness overcame me, like the time Uncle Beckett and I left the mall after Christmas shopping and discovered his car had been broken into. Unlike me, Uncle Beckett kept his car unnervingly clean, so the would-be thieves didn't find much. The thought of our house being robbed was a much scarier proposition than a car. The screen door was open far enough that it touched the black iron handrail at the top of the stoop. We always kept the screen door closed to keep the mosquitos out of the house.

I sucked in a deep breath and plodded up the front steps, my feet heavy as if I was wearing my Doc Martens instead of flip flops. To my surprise the side door was ajar. Through the opening, I saw Cher sitting upright on a kitchen stool staring intently at the door. Thankfully, she hated the outdoors, so she would never make a run for it.

I planned to come home, grab my duffel bag, and leave within a ten-minute window, but upon seeing the kitchen, I knew my exit wouldn't be that simple. The breakfast dishes were still piled in the sink, every cabinet door stood open, and a basket of dirty laundry sat on the kitchen counter.

"Aunt Delia?" I called in a loud whisper. "Are you here?"

I was frightened. I had never seen the kitchen in such disarray. I picked up my aunt's rolling pin, afraid an intruder would jump out at any moment. Cher released a low growl and bounded off the chair into the dining room, as if she wanted me to follow. I took off my flip-flops and tiptoed behind her.

The dining room had two archways on either side, and from where I stood, I could see the door of Uncle Beckett's study. My heartbeat quickened when I saw his study door open, because Aunt Delia ordered my uncle to keep it closed. She said guests shouldn't see a room with piles of books and papers scattered on the floor after they eat. I continued my tiptoe trek across the dining room, still clutching the rolling pin in my right hand. The slamming of desk drawers and a book hitting the floor echoed from inside the room. I wiped the perspiration from my forehead with my arm.

I inched through the dining room with my back to the wall and raised the rolling pin above my head before stepping into the doorway of the study.

I screamed and dropped my makeshift weapon, leaving a small dent in the hardwood floor. "Aunt Delia!" I yelled.

She put her hand on her chest like she had just been shot and fell to her knees.

"Gwyn," she said, noticeably startled.

In eighteen years, I had never seen Aunt Delia stunned, but in two days I had seen her surprised twice, and it scared me.

"I'm sorry, I, uh," I stammered, "The door was open and the kitchen a mess. I thought someone broke in."

We stared at each other for a few moments before Aunt Delia stood. She smoothed her dress. I reached down for the rolling pin.

"I was just looking for—" she paused and inhaled sharply. "I was looking for an insurance policy."

Aunt Delia turned away from me and picked up the Santa Claus pencil sharpener I gave Uncle Beckett for Christmas as a six-year-old. She wiped the dust from Santa with the hem of her skirt and returned him to the desk.

"An insurance policy?" I asked.

"Yes, Nana Lola and Papa Clive's health insurance policy. Beckett always kept a copy. He asked me to get it for him."

Apparently, I wasn't the only one good at lying. I decided playing along would be safer than calling her bluff.

"Why does Uncle Beckett need you to send him the papers? Wouldn't Papa Clive have the policy at the house?" I asked, mustering up a voice of calm curiosity.

"You know your uncle; he is so particular. He wants his own copy."

Aunt Delia closed all the desk drawers and replaced several books on the shelf.

I stepped back into the dining room as she left the study, closing the door behind her. She grabbed the rolling pin from my hands and tapped it against her palm a few times, followed by a deep breath and a long exhale.

"Well, it looks like I have some dishes to do," she said.

I ran to my room and rummaged through my closet for the shoebox that contained Adam's letter and the wedding photograph. I put the box into my backpack and the backpack into my duffel bag.

Every fiber of my being screamed that Aunt Delia would come for my room next.

21
FAIRY TALES

"Gwyn, could you hold still? Do you want mascara all over your face?" Denise placed one hand on my knee to stop my leg from bouncing and leaned in to coat my eyelashes with mascara with the other.

"Sorry, I'm not used to other people covering my face with makeup." I forced a grin.

"Stop smiling and close your eyes. I want this to be perfect."

"Why are you so into all this? It's a wedding reception; no big deal."

"No big deal?" Denise stood back to admire her work. "It's not every day that my best friend can be a real-life Cinderella."

"I wouldn't go that far. Isaac could be Prince Charming disguised in Birkenstocks, but I'm no chambermaid, thanks to you." I admired Denise's handiwork in the mirror.

"Maybe not, but you've got someone to play the role of evil stepmother." Denise smirked.

"Let's not start talking about Aunt Delia. I'm nervous enough as it is." I stepped into my slip and unzipped the garment bag that contained the dress Veronica had lent me.

"Okay, I'll stop talking about her after I ask you one question," Denise said.

"Fine, what is it?" I turned to face her.

"Was it just me, or was your aunt totally freaked when you opened that ring from your uncle?"

I turned my back to her and removed the garment bag from the hanger. "Um... I didn't notice anything."

Denise grabbed me by the shoulders and spun me around.

"You're lying, I can tell," Denise said firmly. "You might be able to fool adults, but I see right through you. Give me details, girl —details."

I began to cover my face with my hand, but Denise grabbed my wrist before I made contact. "Don't mess up my masterpiece." She leaned in inches from my face to insure I hadn't done any damage.

"Still looks good," she said, sounding relieved. "Now, tell me what's up with the ring."

"Fine, but don't breathe a word of this to anyone," I said.

"Pinky-swear." Denise locked her pinky finger with mine.

"The ring belonged to Catherine, Uncle Beckett's first fiancée. It was her engagement ring."

"What?" Astonished, Denise dropped the mascara tube on the floor. It rolled under her desk. She dropped down onto her belly and reached under the desk with her right arm. I waited for Denise to retrieve the wayward makeup before continuing.

"Uncle Beckett told me about her before he left for Delaware. She died in a car accident before they got married. He was completely in love with her."

"Oh my God, that's horrible." Denise flopped down on the bed hard enough that the springs creaked.

"There's more. You know that shoebox I found with Brenda Quigley's picture?"

"Uh huh."

"The ring was in there. I don't know why, but it was. Aunt Delia must have hidden it. Anyway, Uncle Beckett thought he had lost the ring. Once I knew who it belonged to, I couldn't keep it. So, I put the ring and a note in his car before he left."

"And then he gave it to you for your birthday."

"Yep, and that means Aunt Delia knows someone found the shoebox. I caught her rifling through Uncle Beckett's study this afternoon."

Denise shook her head. "She thinks he found it."

"I'm going to have to tell her the truth. I can't let her believe Uncle Beckett is hiding something from her."

Denise put her hands on my shoulders and studied my face. "No wonder you're so tense. Listen, tomorrow we'll figure out how to tell her."

"Thanks." I hugged her tightly. "I'm not sure what I'd do without you, Denise."

"And I'll go with you when you do. You don't have to face life alone, you know."

"That sounds like something Isaac would say."

"He's a smart guy," Denise said. "Look, you go out and have a fabulous evening. We'll have plenty of time to figure this out when we're painting tomorrow."

Denise held up the gallon of paint and a new roller.

"You don't ever get stressed out, do you?" I asked.

"One of us has to stay calm, and God knows you aren't capable of that."

I rolled my eyes.

"I saw that," Denise said before digging through my duffel bag. "Okay, so what bra did you bring to wear."

"Um, you packed my bag, remember?"

"A little sarcastic, aren't we? I thought you could handle your underwear at least."

"I guess I can wear this one." I glanced down at the pale blue bra I wore and then at my best friend's disapproving expression.

"With that dress? You need a strapless. I can't believe you don't own one."

"I don't. I never had a reason."

"Go put this one on." Denise handed me a nude bra and motioned me toward the bathroom. "And I better be the only one who sees you in it tonight." She smirked and hit me on the bottom with a towel before I could close the bathroom door behind me.

I MET up with Isaac twenty minutes late. When I was nervous, I tended to drive under the speed limit and tonight, I counted at least five cars passing me on the road. Isaac had given me directions to a historic house on Route 5 on a two-lane road between Riverbend and Richmond. I leaned over the steering wheel so I could better see the road signs. Two dozen balloons tied to the fence lining the entry leading to the house signaled I had arrived at the right place.

Before getting out of the car, I slipped on Catherine's ring, which I had been hiding in my glove compartment. Isaac stood alone on the porch in a tuxedo with a white rose boutonniere pinned to the lapel. He smiled and waved as I approached.

Isaac embraced me at the foot of the stairs. "I thought you would never get here. Veronica's friends were starting to believe you didn't exist."

"Sorry, I have no good excuse, unless you count slowing down for a gaggle of geese to cross the road."

Another car pulled into the gravel parking lot spotted with large pine trees. I surveyed the large yard that enveloped the house.

"Are we out in the middle of nowhere or what?" I asked.

"At least we won't have to worry about disturbing the neighbors." Isaac pointed to the dancing silhouettes of the guests behind a large window. "God, I'm glad you're here."

I squeezed him tightly around the waist, resting my head against his chest. He kissed my forehead.

He leaned back to get a full view of my head. "What's this?"

"A birthday gift from Denise. What do you think?" I flipped my hair with my hands. "Too much?"

"I'd like you no matter what color your hair was," Isaac said with a broad grin.

"Good answer." I ran my hands through his auburn curls. Over his shoulder, his family and friends laughed and hugged one another inside the brightly lit house. I wondered how my reserved family would react to another family so unafraid to show affection. The movement of shadow and light through the windows so mesmerized me that I didn't notice Isaac staring at me.

"You look beautiful, by the way."

"Thanks." I turned away from Isaac's gaze. I was never good at accepting compliments.

"Hey, look at me," he said, cradling my cheeks in his hands and pressing his lips against mine.

I closed my eyes and breathed in the scent of his cologne, intermingled with the lavender and rosemary bushes that surrounded the house.

"Are you ready to go inside and face my family, or do you want to make a run for it?"

"Running away is tempting." I smiled and squeezed his hand. "But I don't want to be the reason you are disowned."

"Yeah, that would be bad," Isaac said, chuckling.

"Come on, I love your parents. They're much more fun than my family." We locked arms before walking up the porch stairs.

"But you don't have to live with them," Isaac said. "My parents are embarrassingly free-spirited. And on the record, I'm not responsible for any personal questions they ask you."

"I'll only hold you accountable if you leave me to answer them alone."

"Never." He kissed my temple before opening the door and flooding the porch with the light from the foyer.

"She's here!" Mrs. Quigley yelled, pushing her way through the houseful of guests as if I was the only guest she was waiting for. She hugged and kissed me on both cheeks. "Don't you look beautiful, Gwyn. Isn't she beautiful, Isaac?"

Isaac wrapped his arm around my waist. "Yes, she is."

"I'm sure your mother took loads of pictures of you before you left," Mrs. Quigley said. "I never miss the chance for a picture of my children all dressed up."

"Actually, no ma'am, I got ready at Denise's," I said. "My mom's at work."

"Well, then, we'll have to make sure she gets a picture." Mrs. Quigley turned toward her husband, who spun pineapple chunks in the chocolate fountain. "Steve, would you find the photographer?"

"Sure," the man said before pulling the last piece of fruit from the skewer. "Gwyn, we're glad you're here."

"Thanks, Mr. Quigley. I'm glad too."

Isaac's resemblance to his father was immediately recognizable, with the exception of his eyes. They both had the same tall and lean build and thick auburn hair. Mr. Quigley's skin appeared to have a permanent tan, like one of those lifeguards on a TV movie, except I know Mr. Quigley's came from working on the farm and not a bottle.

"Now you two come stand in front of this lovely fireplace." Mrs. Quigley led us to a room off the main foyer, speaking to several guests by name as we passed, most of whom, thankfully, didn't look familiar. Ever since I saw Old Ruthie, I was paranoid about running into one of Aunt Delia's friends. Mrs. Quigley led us into a ballroom, which was grand without being overly pretentious. Each wall had white beadboard up to the level of the chair rail. Above the beadboard, 1920s Art Deco wallpaper adorned with flying cranes surrounded the room.

Mrs. Quigley wore a charcoal-gray, floor-length gown that suited her frame. I could tell she had once been an athlete by the definition in her arms. As she turned her back to us to arrange the flowers on the stone mantle, the right strap of her dress slipped down her shoulder, revealing a tattoo of two sparrows.

"Like my mom's tattoo?" Isaac whispered in my ear.

"Sure, just a little surprised."

I had never seen a tattoo on a woman over forty. When Isaac's mom turned around, she caught me staring.

"What are you whispering about?" Mrs. Quigley asked as she absentmindedly adjusted the strap on her dress.

"Your sparrows, Mom," Isaac said with a giggle.

"Oh those." She blushed. "I had them done after Isaac was born. One for each child."

"Vee and I used to tease her that if Mom had another child, she could add bird poop to represent the new kid."

"That's terrible, Isaac," I said.

"Don't mind my son's jokes, dear," Mrs. Quigley said, glaring at Isaac before breaking into a smile. "See, after him, who in their right mind would have another?"

"Mom." Isaac covered his face in embarrassment.

"I'm kidding, baby." She pinched his cheek, which seemed only to make the situation worse. I wrapped my arm around Isaac's waist and squeezed.

"Thank God, Dad's here with the photographer." Isaac clapped his hands loud enough it made me jump, then laugh. Veronica and

Chris followed behind Mr. Quigley. Veronica looked effortlessly radiant in a strapless knee-length dress with a belt of pearls. She wore her braided hair like a crown, with another string of pearls woven through the braid. If she had wings, I would have thought her a fairy.

"There you guys are." Veronica collected both of us in a hug. "Gwyn, you remember Chris?"

"Of course, nice to see you again." I smiled at Chris, and he nodded.

Chris wore a tuxedo perfectly tailored to his frame. The pastel yellow pocket square added a perfect splash of color.

Mrs. Quigley waved her arms, hoping to move us along. "Well, let's get on these pictures. First, we'll take some just of the two of you. Come on, stand right here."

Neither Isaac nor I enjoyed being the center of attention. Beads of perspiration gathered on my neck as three overly giddy faces stared at us. The photographer adjusted the position of our heads. After the tenth photo, Isaac and I attempted to make our escape.

Mr. Quigley grabbed his son's forearm. "Oh, no, you don't. We want one of the four of you. Chris and Vee, go up there with them."

Veronica put her arm around my shoulder and squeezed. She radiated with joy.

"And after that, we can take one of the whole family," Mrs. Quigley said, clasping her hands together.

After another dozen photos, the photographer left the room to accost other unsuspecting guests. My field of vision flooded with what seemed like a hundred floating red dots. I steadied myself on Isaac's arm.

"Now you aren't going to let this beautiful girl get by without dancing, are you?" Mr. Quigley asked his son.

"Dad, you know I don't like dancing. She's welcome to go if she wants though." Isaac looked at me, and I winced.

"Oh, we can't have that, little brother. It's my reception, and you're dancing with us." Veronica grabbed Isaac and me by the wrists before we could protest and pulled us across the hall and onto the hardwood dance floor with at least fifty of their closest friends and family members.

22
RESOLVE

"See, that wasn't so painful, was it?" I said, nudging Isaac with my elbow as we strolled to my car.

"Not too bad," Isaac responded, "if you don't count my cousin's six-foot-five date trying to limbo, and my mother ordering the photographer to follow us around all night."

"I'm sure that won't be the last time your mom chases us with a camera."

"Now that, you can count on." He stopped and wrapped his arms around my waist. "You know my family really likes you. I think if we ever broke up, they would keep you and kick me out."

"Ah, well, don't go getting any ideas," I said.

Isaac rested his forehead against mine. "You've got nothing to worry about, promise."

"Even when I go to Boston?"

"Especially then. You'll only be a train ride away."

"Isaac?" I said after several silent minutes.

"Yes?"

"I decided that I'm ready to tell my aunt about us. It terrifies me, but I don't want to keep you a secret anymore."

"It's a little terrifying for me, too, but the longer we're together, the harder it will be to keep it from her. That's a lot of pressure on both of us, and on your friends too."

"I know. I don't want anyone to feel like they have to keep my secrets, especially you."

"Gwyn, I knew what I was getting into. Remember I'm the one who invited you to our house in the first place and encouraged you to get information from my mom. We're equally to blame."

"I don't know about that." I twisted Catherine's ring around my finger. "Maybe if my aunt was easier to talk to, things wouldn't have gotten so out of control."

"Would you like me to be with you when you talk to her?"

I nodded.

"I plan to tell her after work on Monday."

"It's going to be okay, Gwyn," Isaac said quietly. I nuzzled my cheek against his chest, and he wrapped his arms tightly around me.

"I wish I could just walk away. I don't know why I need her approval so much."

"Isn't it amazing that no matter how crazy our family is, we still want them to love us, and we would do anything—" His voice trailed off as he gazed at the vast starlit night. My eyes followed his.

"Anything to feel accepted," I replied.

Storm clouds drifted over the bright yellow moon, darkening an already black sky.

THE ROAD SEEMED to barely resemble the one I drove only five hours earlier. The narrow asphalt shoulders were almost invisible as I maneuvered each curve. A light drizzle misted the surface of the road. I eased on the brake. I didn't need a speeding ticket late at night on a road where I wasn't supposed to be. I promised Denise I would return by eleven, and I knew she would grill me for every detail of the night's activities, but exhaustion had set in, leaving me in no mood for excited girl talk.

I debated on whether to turn off the radio. When I experienced anxiety, even the most mundane decisions became monumental. The chatter of the late-night radio deejay was a welcome distraction to my racing thoughts, but how heavily I pressed the gas pedal tended to be in direct proportion to the loudness of the radio. In the end, I left it on. Bono belting "Where the Streets Have No Name" seemed intensely appropriate.

The thought occurred to me that no one knew my location at this moment in time. If I suddenly went missing or drove off the road into a ditch somewhere, would Denise know where to tell the police to look for me? When my family finally found my body, it would be bloated from the late-night rain, my hair caked with dirt, and my eyes— I shuddered at the thought.

I had been cursed with a vivid imagination. Still, contemplating my own mortality was more pleasant than thinking about how to deliver the truth to my aunt Monday afternoon.

At the beginning of the summer, my goal—in my own words— was to make my aunt's life *a little more miserable*. I never planned to reopen old wounds of my aunt's and uncle's broken hearts, and I never planned to fall for someone. Maybe it was best I planned to leave the state. Once the truth surfaced, I probably would be kicked out anyway, most likely without money or a car. Maybe I could go to Boston early, hitch-hiking my way up the Mid-Atlantic States.

I gripped the steering wheel and leaned forward, my chest almost touching the vinyl wheel. It had stopped drizzling, but the wet pavement still glistened in the moonlight. The forecast called for rain all weekend. I flicked off my high beams as an oncoming car approached and passed me.

I glanced at the clock, ten forty-five.

When my eyes returned to the road, a shadowy figure of an animal leapt into the lane not fifteen feet in front of me.

I swerved.

The world around me spun like the teacup ride at the State Fair. My car fishtailed, before sliding off the shoulder of the road and halting to a stop in the mud. My body thrusted forward while, in the same breath, my seatbelt threw me back. Breathing heavily, I looked over my shoulder to see a deer run into the woods. Uncle Beckett had always warned me to watch for animals, but until tonight, I had never come close to hitting one.

Despite not having heard my car hitting another object, my instincts compelled me to inspect for any signs of damage, although I wouldn't know what to do if I found any. I took off my formal shoes and slipped on my flip-flops. Clutching the hem of my dress about my mid-thigh, I stepped out of the car.

Thankfully, the car didn't have so much as a scratch. I breathed a sigh of relief until I saw the space between my front bumper and the tree—a space that would have barely fit my English textbook. I had been saved by the mud that now oozed over the soles of my flip-flops.

There are those moments in your life that only exist to wake you up and shift your perspective. The split seconds that you will remember for the rest of your life.

Here I was, standing in the dark, wearing muddy flip-flops and a formal dress, and thanking God that the worst that could happen didn't. Speaking the truth wouldn't kill me either.

23
HONESTY

"Are you really going through with telling your aunt?" Denise asked as she spread a painting tarp across her dresser, coating the air with the smell of new plastic.

I opened the window for ventilation. The lack of sleep, coupled with the odor, made my head spin.

"I can't let this go on anymore," I said. "Everything's gotten so out of hand. I told you what I caught Aunt Delia doing, right? That she was rummaging through my uncle's things?"

"Yeah, you told me."

"I was afraid she would search my room next, so I brought the shoebox with me."

"Well, I for one will be relieved when you tell her," Denise said.

"Why? What difference does it make to you?"

"Watch the attitude." Denise placed one hand on her hip and pointed her paintbrush at me with the other. Denise could only maintain an angry face for a few moments before she broke into a smile.

"Sorry, I'm a little on edge."

"See, that's what I mean," she said. "You've been so distracted lately. At your birthday party, you hardly said a word. And last night, you didn't tell me anything about your date with Isaac. You just said you were tired and went to bed. That's not like you."

Denise stared at me, waiting for a response, but when I didn't provide one, she continued. "And lately when we talk, it's always about your aunt. You never ask about what's going on in my life."

"Are you done berating me now?" I asked quietly.

"I want my friend back. You're no fun like this." Denise flicked paint on my overalls and ducked, expecting me to retaliate, but I didn't move. "Ah, come on, Gwyn."

"Fine." I playfully charged at Denise with a paintbrush. I drew a smiley face on her shoulder before I hugged her. "I guess I have been a little obsessed with my own problems."

"Ya think?" Denise pursed her lips and raised an eyebrow. "Okay, enough of this serious stuff. You can make it up to me by getting to work."

Denise stirred the sky-blue paint, dipped her brush in the thick color, and began to edge the doorframe. I followed and began to work around the window.

"So how are things going with you and Danny?" I asked.

"Never better. Actually, we've been talking about eloping to Vegas after I turn eighteen in September."

I spun around and looked at her. Her expression was stoic, without an air of sarcasm. I, on the other hand, stood flabbergasted. "Denise, you can't be serious? When were you going to tell me?"

Our eyes locked, and after a few moments a wide grin broke across Denise's face.

"Well, answer me," I insisted.

Denise laughed. "We're not getting married. I just wanted to make sure you were listening."

This time when she flung paint at my overalls, I returned fire. After a few rounds of paint slinging, we both were bent over, half-laughing, half-panting.

"Okay, so you want details about Isaac?"

Denise stood upright, eyes wide and eager like one of those little dogs who hunt rabbits. She held the paintbrush in her right hand. Slow drips of paint plopped onto the plastic tarp, nearly missing her bare feet. "Yes, I'm all ears."

I swallowed hard. "I think I'm in love with him."

Denise released the paintbrush. The silence broke with a clunk and a soft thump as the handle, then the bristles, hit the floor. Her feet, which she had managed to keep paint-free all afternoon, now were spattered with a blue stripe.

24
LIARS

I arrived home from Denise's around dusk. A summer chill descended into one of those evenings where summer forgot it was still July. The developing storm clouds cast a purple hue across the horizon. I held my painting overalls under my arm, and the backpack slung over my shoulder contained Andrew's letters and Adam's portrait. Although I had not let the bag out of my sight, I had not examined its contents in several days. Since meeting Isaac, investigating my aunt's secret had not been my first priority.

I planned to sneak in through the side door and go straight to my bedroom, but when I walked up the stairs to the door and opened it, the kitchen light illuminated my path. Aunt Delia sat with her arms crossed on a stool behind the counter. I had arrived home almost two hours before my curfew; surely, she would let me go to my room with little resistance.

I had barely closed the door when Aunt Delia began questioning me. "Where have you been?"

"I've been at Denise's, painting her room. Mom said she would tell you."

"Yes, that's what your mom told me," Aunt Delia answered without rising from her seat. "But we both know—"

"Who's *we*? We both know what?" My voice rose as I spoke.

"You and me, Gwyn." Aunt Delia placed special emphasis on *Gwyn*. "We both know that you're lying."

"Oh my God, are you kidding me?" I said, dramatically placing the overalls I had been carrying on the kitchen counter and holding up my forearm so my aunt could see the stripe of blue paint that ran the extent of my arm. "I was at Denise's. I can prove it, but I shouldn't have to."

Aunt Delia studied the blue paint splotches and pursed her lips. "Was he with you at Denise's?"

"Who, Aunt Delia—who are you talking about?" My voice lifted in both volume and intensity.

Aunt Delia remained unnervingly calm.

"You know who—the Quigley boy." Aunt Delia's tone was firm.

I swallowed hard, trying to repress the heaviness in my chest. I took a step back.

Aunt Delia leaned forward and placed her hands on the counter. "So, you do know who I'm referring to."

"How do you know about him?" I asked in a low voice.

"I had to find out—in the middle of the produce aisle—who my niece was dating. Mrs. Franklin was happy to give me the details. She told me she saw you and this Quigley boy—."

Aunt Delia waved her hands about as if trying to physically form her thoughts.

"His name is Isaac," I interrupted.

"His name is irrelevant," she said. "Mrs. Franklin told me you attended the wedding reception of this boy's sister, and you were his date. She was so pleased that you were together. I told her such a thing was impossible because you had not told your family."

Aunt Delia stood and stared at me without blinking for a long moment.

"You made a fool out of me, Gwyn," she finally said.

"Aunt Delia, I did not mean for you to find out like that. I'm so sorry."

I stepped forward and put my hand over hers, only to have Aunt Delia snatch it away.

"He's a wonderful person," I continued, "and his family, they are wonderful too."

"I don't like being made a fool, Gwyn. You should have told me the truth."

"Just so you could stop me? I like him, Aunt Delia. I'm eighteen now. I'm mature enough to make my own decisions."

"Do you call lying mature?" She threw her hands in the air and turned her back to me to face the kitchen window. "You are so ungrateful."

The streetlamp's glow brightened the side yard. I made eye contact with the glowing eyes of a large rabbit before he jumped out of view. My gaze shifted to the back of my aunt's head as she tightly gripped the edge of the kitchen sink.

"Aunt Delia, why are you saying this?" I said, tears welling in my eyes. "I have been a good student. I've never got in trouble at school. I deserve to be happy."

Aunt Delia spun around and waved her right pointer finger. "Gwyn, I am not going to stand by and see you ruin your life."

"Ruin my life—with Isaac?"

"If you are sneaking around to see him, I can only imagine what else you have done." Aunt Delia's calm demeanor finally began to break. "So, have you? Tell me the truth."

"Tell you what?"

By the look on Aunt Delia's face, I suddenly understood what she meant.

"Oh my God, are you talking about sex?" I said.

"Well?"

"I've known him for less than two months. No, Aunt Delia, nothing has happened."

"Well, I don't know any more with you, Gwyn."

"You know I'm responsible," I said. "And anyway, Isaac is not like that. He is kind. He would never take advantage of me."

"I forbid you to see him anymore, and you must call Mrs. Franklin and say you are not dating him. That she was mistaken."

I wiped tears from my eyes. "I am not going to lie about our relationship."

"You already did—to me." Aunt Delia placed a clenched fist over her heart.

"Fine, while we're telling lies—" I shuffled through the front pouch of my backpack. "I believe this is yours."

In a bold move, I tossed the envelope across the counter that contained the letter about Andrew's wedding.

Aunt Delia's face grew red. She banged her fist on the table and pointed to the door. "Get out of my house. Now," she said, carefully enunciating each word. "Go."

She pointed to the door, her hand trembling.

I grabbed my keys and ran into the rain, the screen door slamming shut behind me. I got into my car and drove out of town.

25
THE TRUTH

What do we live for, if not to make life less difficult for each other? —George Eliot

*A*fter driving around for an hour, I found myself on the Quigley's doorstep when most Riverbend residents were settling in to watch the late-night news. Cold and drenched with rain, I didn't have the nerve to ring the doorbell. This is not how I wanted Isaac or his family to see me, but I had lost my urge to run further. I knew I was in the right place. Under less intense circumstances, Denise would have been my go-to, but I needed to keep my emotions close and my family protected. Our situation would be prime gossip, the dignified Delia kicking out her only niece. Denise's mom would be unable to keep this one bottled. Everyone in town knew that if you wanted a secret kept, not to tell Eileen Prescott.

I stared at the rectangular stained-glass window in the middle of the Quigley's door, watching droplets of rain etch patterns in the colored glass. My red shorts and vintage Wonder Woman T-shirt clung to my body, and I was crying. The blue paint that once stained my forearm now dotted my black flip-flops. I looked ridiculous.

The lights were on in the house. Taking in a deep breath, I rang the doorbell. Shadows moved to turn on more lights in the living room. Muffled voices drifted through the closed door, and the door vibrated as footsteps approached.

Mrs. Quigley opened the door. I fell into her arms, and she held me. She let me heave, my tears dotting her shirt, and held me like I had never been held before. We stood in the foyer with the front door open, as the rain continued to fall.

Mrs. Quigley did not push for answers. In fact, she had not said a word since opening the door. She held me and stroked my wet hair. Without leaving her embrace, I glanced upward to see Isaac standing in the middle of the living room with pained eyes. Mrs. Quigley turned when she saw me lift my head and motioned for Isaac.

"Take her, Isaac," she said and released me. "I am going to find some dry clothes for Gwyn in your sister's room." She closed the front door and quietly left the room.

Mrs. Quigley's embrace was seamlessly replaced by Isaac's. He placed one hand on the small of my back and the other at the base of my neck, pulling me to him. He kissed the top of my head. My forceful cry had stopped, leaving only light, disconnected tears.

For that moment, Isaac felt like home.

"Thank you," I whispered.

Isaac pulled back, held my shoulders, and gazed into my eyes. With his thumb, he wiped away a tear from my cheek.

"You're safe now," Isaac said.

Isaac rested his forehead on mine. His breath warmed my skin. My rain-soaked shirt had made wet patterns on his faded navy Polo.

"Aunt Delia kicked me out of the house. She said she didn't want to see me ruin my life, so she told me to get out."

"That's heavy stuff." Isaac placed his hands on my sides. "I'm so sorry."

I wiped newly formed tears with my hand. I didn't want to cry again. "By ruin, she meant you—like you'll ruin me. She thinks I'll have a baby and drop out of college or something."

"Gwyn, it's okay. You don't need to explain." Isaac audibly exhaled, and I could feel his heart rate accelerate.

Mrs. Quigley entered the living room carrying a laundry basket. "Here are some fresh clothes, dear."

"Mom, Gwyn's aunt kicked her out of the house," Isaac said.

"Oh my God, honey." Mrs. Quigley gripped my elbow. "Did you have an argument?"

"Yes, over Isaac," I said. "One of her friends saw us at Veronica's reception and told my aunt. I hadn't told her we were together. I've never seen her that angry."

I rubbed my forehead firmly, hoping to ease my emerging headache. "I said some terrible things too—"

Mrs. Quigley drew in a sharp breath. She stared at me as if she could read my thoughts.

"You will stay here tonight in Veronica's room." Mrs. Quigley handed me a stack of clothing and patted me on the back. "Does your mother know what happened, and your uncle?"

"My mom is working the night shift at the hospital, and my uncle's mother is very ill. He's in Delaware visiting her."

"Okay, sweetie." Mrs. Quigley stroked my face. "Go get changed, and we can talk."

The walls of Veronica's bedroom were a soft yellow, and the windows were dressed with white eyelet curtains. Family pictures in chrome frames lined the top of the dresser. One was a church directory picture, and all four Quigley's wore matching shades of green. Isaac appeared to be about eight. They looked happy. Another picture—of Veronica riding the family's quarter-horse, Father Rigsby—sat next to a picture of Veronica and Isaac dressed as Minnie and Mickey Mouse for Halloween. Issacs's mouse-ears were so large, his eyes were barely visible. Minnie dwarfed the toddler-sized Mickey. I had to smile.

I draped my wet clothes over the shower curtain rod in Veronica's bathroom and pulled on the flannel drawstring pajama pants and high school volleyball T-shirt that had been laid out for me. I gazed at my reflection in the mirror and winced. Mascara was smeared all over my face, and the purple eye shadow I had so expertly brushed on that morning had become splotchy. I opened the bathroom drawer and found an elastic hairband and wound my hair into a ponytail. I splashed water on my face and removed my makeup with the washcloth that had been left on the counter. This would be Isaac's first time seeing me without makeup.

I heard a knock on the bedroom door.

"Gwyn, are you okay in there?" Isaacs's comforting voice allowed me to exhale fully.

"Yes, I'll be right there."

When I opened the bedroom door, he stood waiting for me in the hallway.

"I see you changed your shirt too," I said.

"Yeah, some girl got me soaking wet." He grabbed me around the waist and kissed me. "Are you feeling better?"

I nodded. "Hey, Isaac, could you get my backpack out of my car? It's in the trunk." I handed him the key.

"My mom is waiting for you in the living room. It's going to be okay. My mom, she's great at this—being a mom, I mean." Isaac squeezed my shoulder. "I'll be right back."

I stepped into the living room just as the front door slammed shut.

"Mrs. Quigley, I hung my wet clothes over the curtain rod in the bathroom," I said.

"That's fine. Come sit by me, and please, call me Brenda." She patted the cushion next to her on the sofa. She had a large forest green photo album on her lap. I sat down next to her.

"Mrs. Quigley, I mean Brenda, thanks for letting me stay here tonight. I'm sure when Mom gets home, Aunt Delia will let me come back." I glanced at the wooden clock on the mantelpiece, as the clock hands swung past midnight.

"Would you like to talk about it?" she asked.

I nodded and took a deep breath. Brenda smiled and patted me on the knee.

I needed a mom like Brenda right now, not a fun sisterly mom, but one that would chase the monsters away. Her soft, kind eyes encouraged me to tell her everything. I told Brenda about wanting to go to school in Boston, and how my aunt disapproved and withheld my college money. I told her about the hidden Valentine cards from Dad, and the ones I found about Andrew. I told her about the day I snuck in the upstairs room without Uncle Beckett knowing and finding her picture and Catherine's ring. I told Brenda the truth about the flower delivery, and how Isaac covered for me. I told her how I fell in love with her family and about the argument with Aunt Delia that had led me here.

Brenda remained silent as I spoke. She only nodded and periodically squeezed my hand. Her eyes never left mine.

Isaac coughed from somewhere behind me. I had forgotten I sent him out to my car. He set the backpack on the floor against the couch, and then stepped back and slid his hands in his pockets. I could tell Isaac had been choking back tears, but a few had escaped.

"Are you okay?" I asked.

"Yeah, I didn't realize things were that"—he searched for the right word—"complicated. You've had a lot to process."

"Not so sure I've done a good job processing, though," I said.

Brenda patted my knee, and I smiled out of reflex. I unzipped my backpack and pulled out the box. I rubbed my fingers over the faded embossed name of Thalheimers. The narrow box couldn't have contained shoes much larger than ballet flats. Maybe Aunt Delia bought new shoes for her wedding or her first day of work. Isaac placed his hand on my back and peered over my shoulder as I opened the box and removed an envelope.

"This is the picture I told you about." I said handing it to Brenda.

She read the words on the envelope that she had written over thirty years ago and took out the picture. She held it reverently; tears welled in her eyes.

"This is the last time I spoke to your aunt." Brenda tapped the picture with her finger. "I can't believe she kept it."

"Could you tell me what happened?" I asked quietly.

Brenda squeezed my hand tightly and took a deep breath.

"Mom, if it's private, I can leave the room," Isaac said.

Brenda looked at her son, then to me. "No, honey, it's okay. Gwyn will probably appreciate you being here."

Brenda turned to face me. "Really, your aunt should be telling you this story, but I know her. She won't do it willingly. But on the other hand, I think if you knew the story, you would better understand Delia."

I nodded. "Thank you."

Isaac's thumb pressed into my shoulder, forcing my muscles to relax.

"I am two years older than your aunt. We were on the high school basketball team together; that's how we met."

"My aunt played basketball?" That fact alone astonished me.

"Yes, and she was very good. I went to Virginia Commonwealth for college. That's where I met Isaac's dad."

Brenda patted Isaac's knee, and he blushed.

I found it endearing that Isaac's mom still could embarrass him.

"Delia and I still talked often during my first two years of college," Brenda said. "We had been very close. I married Steve after my sophomore year, and we finished our degrees together."

Brenda stopped and rubbed her forehead.

"It's okay if you don't feel comfortable telling me this," I said.

Brenda lifted her head to look at me. "No, Gwyn, you need to know." She paused, took another deep breath.

"About two months after Steve and I were married, I believe it was August, Delia called me from a grocery store in a panic. She had tried to drive to Richmond to see me but she was so distraught, she got lost."

This past Friday was the first time I had ever seen my aunt in a panic. She prided herself on being so steadfast.

I ran my hands through my hair, pressing my fingers against my scalp, maybe to massage out the confusion.

"I went to get her," Brenda continued. "I remember I had to skip a summer school class that day to do so. I remember because it was the first class I'd ever skipped."

Brenda gave a slight smile and shook her head. "When I found Delia, I hardly recognized her; the color had drained from her face. I got Delia in the car and drove her back to Richmond to my house. She told me she had broken off her engagement to a guy named Dennis. His dad was some wealthy banker from the city. They had planned—well her parents had planned—for them to get married after Delia graduated from college. She knew her parents would be furious that she called it off, both the engagement and going to college."

Maybe I didn't know my grandparents either. They always

doted on me. I couldn't imagine them disowning their own daughter.

"Her parents agreed to let Delia go to college, but they saw Dennis as her real future security," Brenda said. "I had a feeling Delia didn't really love Dennis, but I couldn't believe she would give up on college. She wanted to be an illustrator."

Brenda's speech grew in intensity and pace. "I pressed her for answers. This was your aunt, we're talking about; she had always been so sure of herself."

Brenda rubbed her knee forcefully with her right hand and stared at the picture.

"What, Brenda?" I pressed. "What is it?"

She grabbed my hand, as Isaac dropped his hand from my shoulder. We both stared intently at his mom. "Gwyn, she was pregnant."

My throat went dry, and my body turned cold. I didn't blink. I turned away, and my eyes landed on a river landscape that hung on the wall by the kitchen. I recognized it as one of my aunt's pieces with her signature in the bottom right corner. Brenda had kept it all these years. Suddenly the oils seemed to melt into an earth-tone puddle, and the wall began to fade. My body tingled.

"Gwyn, Gwyn!" Isaac's alarmed voice pulled me back to reality.

"Huh?" I rubbed my forehead. "Sorry, too much mental overload."

"Do you want some water, sweetheart?" asked a man's deep voice.

Our talking must have woken up Mr. Quigley. He entered the room barefoot wearing dark blue flannel pajama pants and a white T-shirt. His long maroon terry-cloth bathrobe hung open in the front. His thick salt and pepper-colored hair stood up on end.

"No, I'm good. Thanks, Mr. Quigley." My nearly full can of soda, which was probably flat by now, sat on the coffee table but I didn't want to trouble him.

"I was telling her about Delia," Brenda said.

Mr. Quigley shot her a knowing glance.

"If you need me, come get me, okay?" Mr. Quigley said before leaving the room. I grabbed Brenda's arm. "Please finish your story."

"Are you sure? If it's too much, we can finish tomorrow after you get some sleep."

"I promise, I'm good now."

"Okay, um, she was pregnant," Brenda continued. "And scared. If Delia told her parents, she knew she would be sent away and lose the chance to attend college."

"Did Grandma and Grandpa ever know she was pregnant?"

"Not when she came to me, but they eventually found out. Your mom was so little; she wouldn't remember any of this." Brenda sighed. "Delia told them Dennis wasn't the father, so they sent her away. I never knew where. After she left, I didn't hear from Delia for about a year until she asked me to be with her when she married Beckett. I was the only bridesmaid."

Isaac tightened his grip about my waist. Brenda observed me intently, as if afraid I would faint.

"Don't worry, I'm just processing all of this," I said, taking a sip of soda and cringing at the taste. "Who was the father?"

I couldn't believe those words had left my lips. Who was the father of Aunt Delia's baby? The question would have seemed unfathomable a few short hours ago.

"Now, honey, I don't know. She only said she had a relationship with someone over the spring and summer. Delia never gave me his name. She told me they were in love and that it was his baby."

"Does my uncle know about all of this?" I sat up too quickly and got a head rush. I stroked my temples with my hand.

Isaac held my lower back with his palm.

I waved off Brenda's concerned expression. "Go on, please."

"I assumed she told him, but when, I don't know. Beckett remained quiet during the wedding, but then again, he was always quiet. She never spoke of a baby, and I didn't ask. When they came home from their honeymoon—"

"In Italy," I said. I wanted some of my knowledge about my aunt to be true, but I now wasn't sure of anything.

"In Italy, yes," Brenda said. "When they came home, I never heard anything more. But now with these letters about Andrew, I'm not sure anymore. You see, she never spoke to me after her wedding. I figured I reminded her of a painful time, and she couldn't bear to see me."

"I'm so sorry for all of this." I touched the top of her hand. Brenda put her free hand on top of mine. "I understand now. I saw that sadness in your eyes at the Fourth of July party, when you first found out I was Aunt Delia's niece."

"I never forgot her, Gwyn." Brenda patted my knee. "I am so glad you came to us."

"Me too," I said. "I think I know who the father was."

I reached into my backpack and pulled out the portrait of Adam and the last letter he wrote to Aunt Delia. I handed both to Brenda.

She held the letter carefully like it was a precious artifact. "Yes, I think you are right, Gwyn. The dates line up."

"Mom, do you know who he is?"

Isaac's words startled me. He had been silent for so long, I thought he had fallen asleep.

Brenda shook her head. "No, I don't. I'm sorry."

"There are still so many unanswered questions," I said. "Who is this Adam, and is Andrew their son, or someone else entirely? Did Uncle Beckett know, and if so when did he find out? Did they even go to Italy?"

I paused and took a deep breath "My mom was only six then and didn't know what was really going on. Aunt Delia lied to all of us."

I surprised myself with my words.

Lied to all of us.

The most pious person I knew had been keeping the biggest secret of all.

"It was a different time, Gwyn," Brenda said, shaking her head.

I remembered Uncle Beckett telling me something similar when he showed me Aunt Delia's paintings.

"If a young girl found herself pregnant and unmarried, especially in a small town," Brenda continued, "her life as she knew it was over."

I glanced at Isaac and back at Brenda.

"That's why she was so angry with me tonight," I said. "She feared the same thing would happen to me. Aunt Delia couldn't go to college because of the baby."

My mind raced. "But I'm responsible. She should know that about me."

"I know she should, honey." Brenda patted my knee. "And I think you are exactly right. She sees herself in you. Beautiful, intelligent, the whole world in front of her, and in love."

Brenda raised my chin to meet her eyes. I could only imagine Isaac's expression behind me; he hadn't heard this particular truth. Isaac reached for my hand and interlaced his fingers in mine.

"Even the deepest hidden secrets find their way to the surface," Brenda said, releasing a long, slow breath. "When you make a vow to forget, it's a promise to yourself that you never will."

We sat in silence for several minutes. Truth hung in the air, thick like after a thunderstorm, when dampness feels both heavy and cleansing.

"Oh my, it's almost three A.M.," Brenda said, finally breaking the stillness. "Honey, you need some sleep. The sheets on Veronica's bed are clean." She squeezed my shoulder.

"And you"—Brenda turned toward Isaac—"didn't bother to put your sheets in the dryer. You just have a bare mattress." Brenda tossed her son a couch pillow, which he caught squarely in the stomach.

Isaac rolled his eyes."I know, I know. The sleeping bag is in the closet." Isaac wrapped his arm around his mom's waist and shook his head. "I love you, even when you embarrass the crap out of me."

She winked. "That's what moms are for."

26
MORNING

The white eyelet curtains did little to block out the bright morning sun. I turned away from the light. Isaac was on the floor lying on his side, propped up on his forearm looking at me.

"Hey, Gwynnie."

"Hey." I smiled. "What time is it?"

"It's after eleven."

"You're kidding. I'm late for work—and Mom." I shot up and threw the sheet and blanket away from my legs. Isaac put his hands on my knees.

"Whoa, calm down," Isaac said. "My mom called your mom. She explained that you had an argument with Aunt Delia and convinced her not to come over to our house this morning, that you needed sleep. She called Mrs. Jenkins too; she told her you were sick."

I exhaled deeply and collapsed on the bed. The emotional weight of last night caught up to me. Even on holidays, I typically didn't sleep in, but another wave of exhaustion threatened to overcome me.

"One thing's for sure," Isaac said. "I don't want to be at your house right now. I can only imagine what your mom said to Delia. Your mom was furious."

"Yeah, it's better I stay here," I said. "Brenda didn't tell her everything, did she?"

"No, she only told your mom that you were kicked out because of me."

"Great, now everyone thinks you are bad news."

Isaac playfully pinched my knee.

"Don't start," I joked.

Isaac laughed.

The unzipped sleeping bag was spread out on the hardwood floor in front of the closet. Three sofa cushions were haphazardly thrown on top of it along with a blanket not nearly long enough to cover him. "Did you sleep down there all night?"

"Most of it. I won't lie; it wasn't very comfortable." Isaac rubbed his neck. "My dad keeps the air conditioning so cold, and that sleeping bag isn't meant for arctic temperatures. Vee's room is the warmest in the house."

"Oh, so that's the only reason, the cold." I pursed my lips not totally believing his rationale.

"Well, I also wanted to make sure you were okay." He looked up at me making the most convincing puppy dog eyes he could muster, "Is that so wrong?"

I slipped down on the floor next to him with my legs stretched forward. My heels rested on the interior of the sleeping bag. It really was a thin layer of fleece, maybe intended for summer camping. While I loved the outdoors, I'd never been camping in my life. It would have to be winter camping, I hated humidity, and so did my curly hair. We would have to get better sleeping bags. A shiver traveled from my neck down to my feet. The word *we* slipped into my thoughts so effortlessly. I slid my arms around his waist.

"I think I love you," I said.

"Think or know?" Isaac leaned his cheek against the top of my head.

"I know." I squeezed him tighter. "Just like Leia and Han Solo."

"Look at you, making a Star Wars reference." Isaac nudged me with his shoulder.

"You can thank my uncle for that." My accelerating heart rate competed with the sound of Veronica's ticking Kit-Cat Klock. The white cat taunted me with her eyes and tail that rhythmically moved back and forth.

"So do you think or know?" I asked. I missed the simplicity of my summer-camp Brian *check yes or no* relationship. You didn't have to explain your feelings; you only had to check whether you had them.

Isaac squinted and tilted his head toward the ceiling, seemingly in deep thought. "I know," he said finally. "I'm sure of it."

We sat in comfortable silence, watching our toes rub against one another. Eventually, I fell asleep on Isaac's shoulder.

I woke up to a knock on the open bedroom door. Brenda stood in the doorway, dressed in khaki shorts that showed off her flawless legs and a cotton peasant top. Besides a glimpse of gray hair, no one would have been able to guess that she was in her fifties.

"I made you two sleepyheads breakfast, or, in your cases, lunch." She motioned for us to come with her.

"Do you mind if I freshen up first?" I asked.

"Of course, I put a new toothbrush in the bathroom for you, Gwyn."

"Thanks, Brenda."

I ENTERED the kitchen as Brenda placed pancakes on two plates at the kitchen table. A plastic syrup bottle sat in the middle of the table along with a carton of orange juice, no china bowls or glass pitchers in sight.

"Sit here, at the head of the table, next to Isaac." Brenda tapped the table.

I sat down and reached for the syrup. Isaac had almost finished a stack of pancakes already. Before he could take his last bite, Brenda plopped two more on his plate.

"I've never seen anyone eat quite like my son." She patted him on the back, and he rolled his eyes, unable to reply with his mouth stuffed with pancakes.

"When he brought me lunch at the florist, it was enough to feed a family of five, and that's only what he brought for himself," I said, pinching Isaac's cheek "But you're still so cute."

Isaac dropped his fork, shooting me a mock-stern look. He tried to tickle me.

"Okay, okay, that's enough," I said, laughing.

"You two are perfect for each other—equally as mature," Brenda said. "Oh Gwyn, I washed and dried your clothes for you."

Brenda entered the small laundry room off the kitchen and removed my shorts and T-shirt from the dryer. Brenda laid my clothes over one of the kitchen chairs. "I went to the store this morning and got you these." She held up a package of Hanes women's underwear and reached across the table to hand me the package.

"Oh my God, Mom! Don't embarrass her." Isaac's cheeks flushed crimson.

"You mean embarrass you, Isaac," Brenda said. "What do you expect me to do, send her home without clean things to wear?"

Brenda turned to me. "I hope I got the right size. I guessed, but I did raise a girl, you know."

"You did well. It's the right size." I tried to contain my urge to explode in laughter, but one look at Isaac's horrified expression, and I could no longer hold it in. I laughed so hard; the orange juice burned the inside of my nose. I grabbed a napkin and covered my face. Brenda also erupted in laughter. She clenched a kitchen chair for support.

"Could you two stop it?" Isaac pleaded. "Mom, I can't take it."

Brenda moved behind Isaac's chair and put her arms around his neck and kissed his temple. "I just love my little boy, that's all, and I love his Gwyn too."

27
AFTERMATH

*A*fter a long day, nothing could rival the feeling of a shower and clean clothes. Still breathing in the remnants of cherry blossom body wash, I stepped out of Veronica's bedroom into the hallway. The sensations of family life met me. Water echoed from the bathroom at the back of the house and the dishwasher in the kitchen. The house smelled of citrus air freshener and cinnamon rolls. Seeing no one in the hall, I made my way to the mudroom that opened into the garage.

Against the wall next to the garage door was a shelf lined with hiking boots and leather sandals. I slipped on a pair of boots that appeared several sizes too big but, compared to the others, were only lightly caked with mud. I assumed they belonged to Isaac or Mr. Quigley. Before trekking to the barn, I wrote on the whiteboard above the shelf: *Went to visit the horses, Gwyn.*

Moisture still clung to the air from last night's rain. My skin became sticky within a few moments of stepping outside.

Father Rigsby grazed near the fence; when I approached, he raised his head and released a snort. He nodded as if pointing to my right side; he knew I was hiding the goods. I removed a carrot that I had shoved in my pocket and held it out to him. CoCo's jealousy got the better of her, and she trotted toward me and nudged my hand for a treat.

I stood on the bottom rail of the fence and leaned over, the top rail pressing into my armpits. I needed to feel some physical pain. After the drama of last night, I woke up numb.

Father Rigsby nudged my arm with his muzzle, staring at me as if acknowledging my grief. His nostrils flared as he exhaled. His stare reminded me of Cher and Pepper when, after a bad day at school, they would snuggle beside me on the couch. Cher searched for Pepper several months after he died.

Pepper was a pedigreed Golden Retriever, another expensive remnant of my parent's short-lived marriage. My dad moved into an apartment that did not allow pets, so the dog came to live with us. I believe the only reason Aunt Delia tolerated Pepper was because he held a pedigree. My aunt liked to tease that my mother had picked out a higher-class dog than a husband. I would pretend to laugh at Aunt Delia's joke, but I always wondered what that made me, as I was a product of the lower-class husband.

I HADN'T THOUGHT about Pepper in a long time. The floppy-eared dog reminded me that I had seen Aunt Delia anxious before. The other time had been ten years ago, in mid-August, about a week before the new school year started. I was eight years old. Aunt Delia had sent me out to pick blueberries in late afternoon for a pie she planned to make. The blueberry bushes lined the back corner of Cousin Georgia's property, about a half a mile from our house. Cousin Georgia lived toward the river on a three-acre lot. In our small town, parents often sent a child out on errands, even to the grocery store with a list and a blank check.

Pepper ran ahead of me a few feet, then stopped and waited for me to catch up, before taking off again. It was a typical humid August afternoon in Virginia, heightened by the overwhelming scent of bug spray that Aunt Delia drenched me in before I left.

The blueberry bushes stood at least six feet high and covered about a thirty-foot strip of my grandparents' backyard. The berries hung in bunches, like raindrops, dense without bending the branches. Pepper weaved between the bushes, chasing anything that moved. I was so focused on picking the amount of berries Aunt Delia had requested that I did not hear the rumbling thunder. Afternoon thunderstorms were common in the summer, but this one came up so fast, I barely had time to take cover under one of the bushes.

I pulled my legs to my chest. My knees, scraped from a tumble off my bicycle a few days before, stung as the rain began to fall. Pepper nuzzled his snout under my arm and whimpered. Thunder clapped, followed by a crack of lightning. I put my hands over my ears and rocked back and forth, singing to myself to distract my thoughts.

Hush little baby don't say a word, mama's going to buy you a mockingbird.

Something fell from the sky and dropped a few feet in front me, a nest with two broken robin's eggs. I screamed. I knew their mom would be sad. I wanted mine now.

And if that mockingbird don't sing, mama's going to buy you a diamond ring.

I thought I heard my name being called, but I was too afraid to answer the voice. I stayed rocking and singing. When the voice called out again, Pepper perked up and began barking fervently. He moved a couple feet forward and turned to look back at me. The sound of my name grew louder as footsteps approached, but I did not raise my head until Pepper prodded me with his nose. I looked up to see Aunt Delia. She stood soaking wet and holding an umbrella over her head. I am sure she ran the entire way, making the umbrella of no use. She held out her hand to me.

"Gwyn, take my hand," she said with panic in her voice.

The thunder clapped louder this time.

"I'm scared."

"I know, honey, but you have to." Aunt Delia's eyes were glazed over with tears. "Grab my hand, and we'll go into Georgia's house to get dry."

I don't think my mom or uncle ever knew what happened that day. My aunt must have felt terribly guilty for sending an eight-year-old out into an approaching thunderstorm, and I didn't want to make her feel worse. Plus, I wanted to forget that nightmare ever happened.

After that day, Aunt Delia began to secretly spoil Pepper. She would tell us, "You baby that dog too much. He's merely an animal," then slipped him bacon when no one was looking. And when Pepper died, I heard her cry in the bathroom, but I never said a word.

FATHER RIGSBY HAD GROWN disinterested in me and found a patch of grass to nibble. I sighed and flicked a spider from the top railing of the fence.

"Gwyn!"

I turned toward the voice. Isaac sprinted across the pasture, his boots creating a sloshing sound with every step. When he reached the fence, he collapsed onto it, panting.

"Isaac, what is it?" I asked rubbing his back.

"Your mom's here. Something happened to your aunt. We have to get back to the house."

"Isaac, what happened?" Heat rose in my cheeks.

"I don't know," he said. "Come on, I told her I would get you."

Isaac grabbed my hand and began to run, pulling me along. I tripped over my too-large shoes, catching myself with my hands before I hit the ground. Isaac skidded to a stop.

"Are you okay?"

"Fine, I'll take these off." I slipped out of the hiking boots and ran barefoot the remainder of the way to the Quigley's back door.

We entered the living room and saw Mom sitting on the couch. I approached to hug her, but she did not rise to greet me, instead she reached out and squeezed my hand. I knew her behavior wasn't out of rudeness but probably the result of the dazed stupor she seemed to be in.

"Are you okay?" She asked.

I nodded and sat down in the armchair across from her. Mrs. Quigley motioned for her son to come with her into the kitchen.

"I'm glad you came here. You've got a good head on your shoulders." She squeezed my hand again. "Sorry, I haven't had much sleep. I got home from my shift and all this happened with Delia."

"What happened, Mom?"

"Your aunt had a car accident this morning." Mom absentmindedly adjusted her ponytail that extended above the closure of her ball cap.

"A car accident? Where?" The tears that had been dormant all morning began to sting my eyes.

"Charlie got the call. Delia called him when she couldn't get me on the phone. He got her to the hospital. She's okay. A couple broken ribs and a badly sprained ankle, but she's okay." Mom glanced at the Quigley's grandfather clock, then to her watch. The clock was still set to standard time. "Gwyn, do you know why she would have been going to the bookshop?"

I dropped my gaze to my knees. "I don't know, Mom." I closed my eyes to try to rid my thoughts of the upstairs room and Aunt Delia's trunk.

"Because Charlie said that's where she was going. She hadn't been there in years. I don't get it. Gwyn, she drove onto the sidewalk and hit a light pole. That is so unlike her."

"Did Charlie tell you what made her run up the sidewalk?" I finally allowed myself to look into my mom's eyes.

"He said Delia claimed she was having a heart attack. The doctors examined her, but they found no evidence of one. She told him the pain made her run off the road." Mom squeezed the bridge of her nose with her fingers.

"What do they think happened then?"

"Doctor Evans said she had a panic attack," Mom said. "A panic attack — Delia? I trust his diagnosis, but I just can't believe it. He wanted to keep her overnight. She's in a lot of pain from the broken ribs. I called Beckett; he's on his way."

I tried to hold back tears. "Mom, this is all my fault. If I had told the truth, none of this would have happened."

Mom stood and kneeled in front of me and placed her hands on my knees.

"This is not your fault, Gwyn. You can't take on this guilt."

"But it is, Mom. That's the one thing I know."

28
HEART MONITOR

My mom left the Quigley's soon after our conversation in order to speak to Dr. Evans before his shift ended. Isaac waited for me to change into the clothes Mom brought me—a denim skirt that fell a couple inches above my knee and a pale blue tank top, which definitely came from her closet. I slipped on my black bracelets and Converse shoes to make me feel less like an Easter egg.

On our way to the hospital, Isaac said very little, which I was thankful for. His eyes never left the road, but he held my hand the entire trip, occasionally rubbing his thumb against my knuckles.

I rested my right temple against the passenger window and counted the mailboxes we passed, anything to suppress the fear rising in my chest.

When we pulled into the parking lot of the small regional hospital, I saw Charlie sitting on the bench outside the automatic doors of the emergency room. He was a good man, and he loved my mom. I wished that, one day, she would be able to accept that. Charlie stood as we approached. He squeezed my shoulder. "Hey, kiddo."

"Hey, Charlie."

"Isaac, nice to see you again." He held out his hand.

Isaac gave Charlie's hand an awkward shake. "You too."

We continued through the automatic doors into the brightly lit hospital lobby. The noise of muffled conversations clashed with the classical music pumped through the speakers.

"How is Gwyn's aunt?" Isaac asked.

"Trisha's in with Dr. Evans right now," Charlie said. "They gave her something for the pain. Her ankle is really swollen too. She won't be able to put much pressure on it for a bit."

Charlie stepped aside for a nurse to pass by with a wheelchair-bound patient. He nodded at the nurse, and she returned a polite smile.

"Physically, she'll be fine, but emotionally, she's really shaken up," Charlie said, rubbing the back of his neck. "I have a feeling this wasn't her first panic attack. I've seen a panic attack or two in my day."

"Charlie was in the Army. He's a paramedic now," I said to Isaac.

I thought about Adam. His death had spared him of living with the trauma of war, but not the loved ones he left behind. They continued living with the heartache years later.

"Maybe when your uncle gets here, he can shed some light on this," Charlie continued. "She's refused to speak to a counselor, and she won't talk to Trisha. She only wants to talk to you."

Charlie placed a soft hand on my shoulder.

Nearby, a young father picked up his son, who tugged at his pant leg. The dad carried him through the double doors that led to the maternity ward. I imagined they were going to see the boy's new baby brother or sister. A pang of jealousy surprised me, and I turned away. I always wanted a sibling. I knew that one day, my parents and my aunt and uncle would be gone, and I didn't want to face that alone.

"It's going to be okay, Gwyn," Charlie said.

"That's what everyone keeps telling me." I shrugged.

"Let's take the elevator. We've got to go up to the fourth floor."

Isaac reached for my hand, and we followed Charlie into the elevator.

Aunt Delia was in a small private room about three doors down from the nurse's station. The lights were off inside, and the curtains were drawn so only a small strip of light could pass through. I entered alone, leaving the door slightly ajar. Treading lightly so as to not startle her, I crossed the room and stopped about three feet from the left side of the bed.

My own shallow breathing and the beep of the heart monitor were the only sounds in the room. Aunt Delia turned her head away from the window and fixed her eyes on the ceiling. After several moments of stillness, she broke the silence.

"How much do you know about Andrew?" she asked, her voice flat.

Andrew had never before seemed like an actual person. He had been only a construct of my imagination, but now hearing Aunt Delia speak his name aloud made him real. My cousin Andrew was real.

"I only know what Mrs. Quigley has told me. I went there last night when you—" My voice dropped, barely loud enough to be heard over the air conditioner.

Aunt Delia's lower lip quivered.

"I mean last night, when I left," I said.

"What did she tell you?"

I took a deep breath, followed by the sensation of overwhelming thirst.

"She said that—" I hesitated, searching my brain for the right words. "She told me that you were pregnant before you and Uncle Beckett married, but it wasn't his child."

My aunt tilted her chin toward the ceiling and squeezed her eyes tightly and then reopened. She appeared to be blinking back tears.

"Aunt Delia, Brenda said you were her best friend. She misses you."

I pulled a tissue from the box on the nightstand and stepped closer to the bed. She appeared so petite in the oversized hospital nightgown. The bed coverings were pulled to her waist.

"Does your mom know about this?" She asked.

I shook my head.

"And Charlie? The doctors?"

"No, Aunt Delia, no one else knows."

"Maybe we can keep it that way," she said sullenly.

"If that's what you want." Aunt Delia nodded.

I had gotten brave enough to rest my hands on the cold metal bed rail. Her chest rose up and down, and about every fourth exhale her breath seemed to catch.

"Aunt Delia?"

"Yes." She maintained her focus on the ceiling.

"I'm sorry I didn't tell you about finding the shoebox, and Andrew's letter. I don't deserve your forgiveness."

She reached out her hand and placed it over mine. She let out a sigh. "What's done is done. Let's not speak of it again."

"Yes, ma'am."

The hospital bracelet hung loosely from her thin wrist. The letters forming *Delia S James* seemed to have sucked the last bit of ink from the printer cartridge. Her name never seemed so weak.

Aunt Delia removed her hand from mine and laid it across her waist. She sighed again, causing her to wince in pain.

"They told me I would forget about him. They promised I would." She turned toward me.

"Who promised you, Aunt Delia?"

"The nuns, the nurses, my parents," she said softly. Her wide blue eyes caused every hair on my arm to stand erect. I held my breath. I was frozen, unable to look away. "They were the ones who lied, Gwyn, because I never could forget."

29
UNCERTAINTY

Isaac stood in the hallway outside Aunt Delia's hospital room. The blinds weren't completely closed, so I could see him shift his weight from one foot to the other as he waited. Isaac seemed to fidget during tense situations. He didn't do idle very well. Knowing someone was willing to feel uncomfortable on my behalf made me feel both warm and vulnerable.

"I'll see you soon Aunt Delia," I whispered. But she had already fallen back asleep.

I tiptoed out the door and closed it gently behind me.

Isaac cleared his throat. "Do you want to talk about it?"

"No, not now."

"Okay, is there anything I can do?"

"Take me home."

"I think I can handle that."

I leaned my head against his chest, and he wrapped his arms around my waist. He still shifted side-to-side. In another setting, we would be slow dancing, but instead we held each other in front of the nurse's station. I caught Serena, the nurse supervisor, watching us. She smiled at me, and I blushed.

Serena was an attractive African American woman in her mid-forties, who always had a fondness for my mom. Serena had encouraged her to pursue a nursing degree. Mom had taken some courses, but she never finished.

"Gwyn," Serena called out to me as she smoothed down her pink scrub top. "Aren't you going to introduce me to your young man?"

Isaac jerked away from me as if we had been caught making out by a minister.

"It's just Serena." I laughed for the first time in twenty-four hours. "Come meet her. She's a friend of my mom's. They've worked together for years." I led him towards the nurse's station.

"Trisha told me that you met a nice young man." Serena leaned over the counter and held out her hand, which Isaac took. She clasped her other hand maternally over his.

"I'm Isaac. It's nice to meet you."

"We all love Gwyn here. We've watched her grow up from a little girl."

"Thanks, Miss Serena," I said.

Serena winked at me. "Well, it's true. I used to hide packs of Hubba Bubba gum for her under the desk. Her Aunt Delia claimed it had too much sugar, so we had to be sneaky." She winked at me. "I've got plenty of stories about this one, Isaac."

"Oh, I bet you do. I'll have to get your number," Isaac said, seeming to be amused.

"I don't need both of you conspiring against me." I wished to divert attention from stories about my precocious childhood. "Before we leave, Isaac, we need to call your mom, so she can drive my car over."

"Honey, use this phone." Serena lifted a black touch-tone phone onto the counter. "Dial nine to get a line out."

"Thank you," he said and dialed.

Serena turned her back to Isaac and leaned toward me. "How did it go in there?" She pointed in the direction of Aunt Delia's room.

"She talked a little." I shrugged. "I could tell she was in pain."

Serena patted my hand. "In time, sweetheart. We'll keep a good watch over her."

"I know you will." I smiled at her. "Serena, have you seen my mom?"

"Oh yes, she wanted me to tell you that she and Charlie went to pick up a prescription for your aunt. She'll meet you at home."

"Thanks."

"Now, is your mama ever going to marry Charlie? He worships the ground she walks on."

"You know, as well as I do, he's probably going to have to wait another five years."

"I know that's right." Serena laughed. "And if that one doesn't work out, there's a line of doctors here waiting in the wings."

I nodded, knowing she was telling the truth.

Isaac hung up the phone and turned toward me. "Are you ready?"

I nodded.

"It was nice to meet you, Serena," he said.

"You too, honey. Now you take good care of her."

Isaac put his arm around my shoulder. "I will. You have my word."

WE ARRIVED at my house at almost dusk. I dug through my purse for the spare house key. Without the bulk of the car key I had given to Brenda, it seemed like I was searching for a foreign object. When my hand touched the key, it felt like a little victory. I needed one of those, no matter how small. Isaac held the screen door open as I turned the doorknob.

"Wait, Isaac, does your mom know how to get to my house?" I asked, turning toward him as I pushed the door forward.

"She said she knew where you lived," Isaac said. "I didn't really ask any questions. Mom's bringing dinner over too."

"That's nice of her." We stepped over the threshold, and I flipped on the light. A hint of Aunt Delia's morning French roast lingered in the air. How quickly things can change. When she drank her morning cup, she had no idea that by the afternoon, she would be in the hospital.

"You know my mom," Isaac said. "Oh, this must be Cher." He bent down to stroke the cat's head as she rubbed against his legs.

"That's her." I opened the cupboard to pull out a bag of cat food.

"Do you need some food, little kitty girl?" I asked as if I was talking to a baby.

I poured the food into her empty bowl, and Cher purred as she ate. Her purr echoed in the silence of the house. No sounds of Uncle Beckett rustling around in his study, the television blaring the evening news, or the loud hum of our aging dishwasher. The quiet was both comforting and unnerving.

Isaac pulled me toward him and leaned back against the counter. He rested his forehead against mine. Cher must have finished eating because she weaved around our legs.

"You've been through a lot in the past twenty-four hours," Isaac said. "Are you sure you don't want to talk about it?"

"I don't even know how to explain what I'm feeling. I need some time to process."

Isaac nodded, seeming to understand.

In the stillness, Isaac's breath tickled my face. I read somewhere that the breath was the window to the mind. The rhythm of someone's breathing could indicate fear, excitement, contentment, and the whole range of human emotions. I wondered if two people could sync their breathing, as if they were a single unit.

"What are you so pensive about?" Isaac asked finally.

"Breath," I said, "Yours, mine. It's the one thing that starts life and ends it."

"That's very heavy."

"Yeah." I reached up and held Isaac's face in my hands.

He kissed my forehead and moved down my cheek until he reached my mouth. We remained suspended, as an electrical pulse surged down my spine. Isaac slowly released his lips from mine. His eyes were closed. I found my favorite spot against his shoulder. I listened as the clock ticked off the seconds.

I pressed my cheek against his chest.

"I made a decision when I visited Aunt Delia," I said. "I wanted to talk to you about it."

"What's that?"

"I decided that I can't go to Boston right now—" my voice trailed off. I couldn't believe I was saying this aloud.

Isaac pulled away and stared at me. "What are you talking about?"

"I need to stay here, just for a semester. Aunt Delia needs me to take care of her."

"Gwyn, do you hear what you are saying?"

I tried to look at him, but quickly diverted my eyes.

"She's going to need a lot of help," I said, my words coming fast. "My mom can't take care of her. She's hardly cooked anything more than grilled cheese. Uncle Beckett has to run the shop. I figure I can defer my enrollment and start in January, or next fall at the latest. I can go to the community college in the meantime."

My mouth seemed to be moving without my control.

Isaac held my shoulders. "Look at me, Gwyn. After how much you fought to get out of this town? After everything, you're going to throw it all away?"

"I'm not throwing it away, Isaac. I will go to college. But this situation is my responsibility."

"If you are doing this out of guilt, you are going to resent her even more."

"I'm not doing this out of guilt," I said, trying to also convince myself.

"Are you sure?"

"That's not fair. You don't know what she told me. I had no idea she had been through so much trauma."

"Then tell me," Isaac pleaded. "Help me understand."

"I can't. She asked me not to."

Isaac combed his hand through his hair and cleared his throat. "Gwyn, taking care of her is not your responsibility."

"Then whose is it? We wouldn't be here if it wasn't for me. Isaac, you've never had the same sort of pressures that I've had."

"What's that supposed to mean?"

"Your parents are perfect. You were always free to make your own decisions with no strings attached."

"God, Gwyn." He put his hand on his forehead and pressed his eyes shut. "I'm sorry if my family isn't messed up enough for you."

We were both breathing heavily now. I ran the back of my hand beneath my eye, hoping to prevent the eruption of tears.

"I'm sorry," he said genuinely. "That was mean of me."

"Isaac, I thought you would be a little more supportive."

"This isn't about me being supportive. I can support you without having to agree with you."

"Is that so?"

"If you stay here, you'll be miserable. I love you too much to see that happen. But, if this is what you want, then I'll support you."

"Thank you."

He placed his hands on either shoulder, and we locked eyes. "Promise me one thing."

"What's that?"

"That you wait a week. Just one week and let this settle. If you still want to send the letter to defer your enrollment, then fine. But promise me you'll give it a little time."

"Okay, I promise." I sighed. "You're right. I probably don't need to make any rash decisions."

We both released one of those post-roller-coaster exhales, the exhales that make you realize you've been holding your breath the entire ride.

"Well, we had our first argument—so much fun," Isaac said sarcastically.

"And I'm sure it won't be the last." I touched his forearm to let him know we'd be okay.

Cher meowed as the kitchen door pushed open.

"Hello? Is anybody here?" Brenda carried in a bag of groceries. She saw us and furrowed her brow, realizing something was wrong.

"Hey, Mom," Isaac said, with an apparent drain in his voice.

"What's going on here?" Brenda studied our faces. "Did something happen between you?"

"We're fine." Isaac said, before taking the grocery bag from his mother and setting it on the counter.

"Okay, then, why don't you go out and get the rest of the groceries. The trunk's open."

Isaac nodded and left.

Brenda stood close to me and put her arm around my shoulders. "Tell me what happened, Gwyn."

We sat down on the stools that lined the counter. I picked up one of Aunt Delia's decorative paper napkins and began to crumple it in my hand.

"We just had our first argument. It's been a bad couple of days."

I squeezed the napkin tighter until the heat built up in my palm.

"I know you've had a rough time lately."

I nodded.

"And you and Isaac, whatever it is, you'll work it out."

"I know. We'll be fine."

"Listen, why don't you go take a break?" Brenda said. "Isaac and I will work on dinner."

She turned as Isaac came through the door holding a roll of paper towels under his chin as he balanced two overly full bags of groceries. He placed the paper bags on the counter with a thud.

"This one has always tried to carry everything at once."

"Why make multiple trips if you don't have to?" Isaac said, out of breath.

Brenda removed the contents of the bag. She handed me a bag of popcorn and a Hershey's bar.

"Your mom and Charlie pulled up while I was outside. He wants to mow the grass before Uncle Beckett gets home."

Brenda removed a box of lasagna noodles from the bag. "Sweetie, go on in the living room. We'll take care of dinner. Now go on."

Brenda shooed me into the living room with a stalk of celery. Isaac winked at me.

Isaac's words still rang in my head. I couldn't believe how, one minute, we were making out, and the next, we were in a fight. Relationships aren't for the weak.

THE SOUND of the lawn mower grew louder, then faded as it passed the window of the living room. I had turned down the volume on the television so low that the banter of *Friends* contributed only a low hum to the room. The screen door opened and shut, and my mother's footsteps and friendly greetings echoed from the kitchen.

Lying on my side, I rested my temple on the arm of the sofa and mindlessly flipped channels, trying to match words with lips.

"Hey, baby, what are you doing here?" Mom asked as she

picked up my feet from the sofa and sat down. She rested my feet on her lap.

"Isaac and I had an argument."

"Is everything okay?"

"It's not a big deal. I'll get over it."

My mom patted my leg.

"You have to expect some arguments in a relationship. The first is always the hardest."

"I don't really want to talk about it right now."

"Okay, but I'll be here when you want to."

I nodded.

"Do you have to go back to the hospital tonight?" I asked.

"Yeah, I told them I would work my shift. Serena didn't want me to, but I would prefer to be there. I can look in on Delia too."

"When is she supposed to be released?"

"Tomorrow afternoon. I'm hoping Beckett will arrive sometime tonight."

"Yeah, me too."

Mom's blond hair sat in a disheveled pile on her head. She drew her legs onto the couch, forcing me to move mine.

"You deserve a mom more like Brenda." Mom fingered her anklet.

"What are you talking about?" I asked, surprised. I turned off the television and dropped the remote on the floor.

"She's in there making dinner for her son's girlfriend's family. If the roles were reversed, I wouldn't know to do that. I'd be lucky to think of bringing over a take-out pizza."

"You're a great mom. I always knew you loved me; that's all that matters. This is stress talking." I leaned toward her and placed my hand on her knee.

"I'm serious, Gwyn," Mom said. "I am no good in a crisis, at least at home. Give me a full hospital waiting room anytime over a family catastrophe."

Mom released a heavy sigh. "Delia handled everything. Look at me, Gwyn. I'm thirty-eight, and I've let my sister be the grown up while I've only screwed around all these years."

"Mom, I've never thought of you that way. I knew you did the best you could. When you married Dad, you didn't know it wouldn't work out. It's okay."

"Your father, that's another thing," Mom said. "How does my daughter, at eighteen, make better decisions about men than I ever did? That guy in there adores you. He's responsible and mature. After your dad, and that string of ridiculous boyfriends in my twenties, you would think I had sense enough to marry the one man I've dated that is stable."

Mom turned the beads on her bracelet so vigorously, I thought one might spin off.

"Did Charlie ask you to marry him again?" I asked quietly.

"Yes, after your birthday party last week. I'm afraid if I don't say yes this time, he'll be gone for good." Mom's gaze shifted to Charlie, who bobbed back and forth outside the living room window as he edged the walkway with the Weedwacker.

"I think you should marry him, Mom. He's a good guy."

"You really think so?" Mom turned to face me.

"I've graduated. I can take care of myself now. You deserve to see what else life has to offer you. You could get married before the summer's over and take a nice honeymoon."

"You're not kidding, are you?"

"No, I'm serious. Especially after all that's occurred today. I mean, you can't wait around for life to happen to you."

"Life definitely happened to us, didn't it, baby?" Mom gently clasped my ankle and smiled. "I suppose it doesn't have to be anything fancy."

"You could go to the courthouse or have the wedding in the backyard. Denise's uncle is ordained. I'm sure he'd be willing to perform the ceremony."

"You really think I should do this?"

"You guys have been together for five years. He loves you."

Mom leaned forward to look at Charlie again through the window. Even from a distance, you could see patches of perspiration on his white T-shirt. He took off his baseball cap and rubbed his forehead with his arm before catching my mom's gaze. He waved, and she smiled.

"Maybe you're right, baby. Maybe you're right."

30
STILLNESS

After my mom left for the hospital, I retreated to my room. Brenda was downstairs cleaning the kitchen. She had sent Isaac to the store for paper towels, because she had already used up three rolls.

I ran my fingers over the books on my shelf until I found Aunt Delia's copy of *Anne of Green Gables*. I knew I would be unable to sleep tonight, so I planned to reread the book for the first time in seven years. I removed the picture of Uncle Beckett that I had tucked behind the cover and laid it on my desk. How I missed him.

A light knock startled me. "I wanted to tell you that Mom and I are getting ready to leave," Isaac said, leaning against my doorframe.

"I didn't hear you come in."

"I can leave if you were in the middle of something."

I laid the novel on my bed. "No, it's all good. I'm looking through some old books."

"So, this is your room, huh?" His eyes moved from wall to wall, and then he proceeded to my desk and picked up each item on the tabletop.

"A little nosey, aren't we?"

"I'm sorry, I didn't mean to," he said, dropping his head in remorse. He carefully set down the picture he held.

I couldn't help but laugh as he handled my plastic picture frame like fine china.

"So why did you come up here?" I asked.

"Well, before Mom and I left, I wanted to"—he took my hand—"to apologize for acting like a jerk earlier."

"Oh."

"I have no right to tell you what to do. It's your decision, Gwyn. You must do what you think is right." He gazed up at the faint green glow of the stars dotting my ceiling.

"Thanks. I really appreciate that." I took his other hand in mine. We were now standing face-to-face.

"Whatever you decide, promise me you will give it a few days. And I'll support you no matter what." Isaac looked at me with those kind eyes. I hoped those eyes would always make me melt.

"I promise."

He lifted my chin. "Hey, I want to take you somewhere fun tomorrow."

"What were you thinking?"

"I don't know, maybe we could go to the beach. Denise and Danny could come with us."

"That sounds good." I tried to sound interested. "I don't want to get back too late. Aunt Delia is coming home tomorrow."

"We can leave early. I have something to do in the morning, but I'll be here right after."

I nodded. "I'll be here."

"Are you going to be alright by yourself tonight? I really don't want to leave you, but my mom needs to get home."

I placed my hand on his chest. "It's okay. I'm just fine by myself."

After Isaac left, I slipped under my comforter. Cher paced in a circle before curling up between my legs.

I managed to read eleven pages of *Anne of Green Gables* before falling into a hard, dreamless sleep.

I COULDN'T REMEMBER the last time I ate breakfast alone. I was still in my pajamas, which consisted of a pair of lightweight flannel pants, even though it was summer, and a ribbed tank top. Cher's purr competed with the tick of the kitchen clock as she wove between the legs of the stool where I sat. I examined my mug and slowly stirred in a teaspoon of sugar. I had terrible coffee-making skills, but I drank it anyway. I imagined myself sitting here on this kitchen stool for the next 365 days, drinking my own bad coffee. I shivered.

The doorknob rattled, and I glanced up to see Uncle Beckett through the window in the door. He fumbled with the key while he balanced a large duffle bag on his shoulder. I slid off the stool and opened the door for him.

"Gwynnie." He smiled, dropped his bag, and wrapped his arms around me.

I squeezed him back. "Hey, Uncle. I missed you."

"Missed you too." He raised his head and sniffed. "Did you make coffee?"

"Yeah, but don't drink it."

"Still haven't achieved the proper coffee-grounds-to-water ratio?"

"Something like that."

"I'll take your word for it." He opened the refrigerator and pulled out the iced tea pitcher. "I can get my caffeine in other ways."

"Charlie made that, so you know it's strong."

"Good." Uncle Beckett poured himself a large glass. "Gwynnie, I just got back from the hospital."

My heart began to race. I did not know what was coming next, but I knew whatever came would be uncomfortable.

"I think we need to talk." He picked up an orange from the fruit bowl and began to peel it.

"Yes, sir." I sat back down, and Uncle Beckett pulled a stool up to the counter and sat opposite of me.

"Gwyn, I don't really know where to begin," he said. "I had always thought we could be honest with each other. But it's obvious now we both have been keeping things from each other."

Uncle Beckett tilted his chin downward and looked at me over the rim of his glasses. I sipped some coffee, but as soon as I swallowed, I held back the urge to vomit. He continued, "You know why your aunt was on the way to the bookshop when she crashed, don't you?"

"Yes, and it's all my fault, Uncle." I raised my eyes to meet his. I couldn't believe I'd been keeping secrets from the man I trusted most.

"Delia only told me that she was driving to the bookshop to look for something, and that you knew about Andrew." Uncle Beckett stared at me, and time seemed to suspend. Even the small particles of light froze in the atmosphere.

I took a deep breath. "God, I don't know where to start," I said. "Everything got so out of hand."

My uncle didn't speak but just stared at me.

"At the beginning of the summer, I was so mad at Aunt Delia," I said. "Then I found this letter in the mail from a woman named Susan, saying that Andrew had gotten married. I don't know what I was thinking. God, I'm just stupid, I guess."

I was sweating so much, my bottom seemed to stick to the stool. I squirmed to release my thighs from the seat.

"That's when I started snooping around and found a shoebox in the upstairs room of your store. It had all this mysterious stuff in it, like a letter from a soldier named Adam and Catherine's ring. I suppose it all snowballed from there."

"You don't need to explain anymore." Uncle Beckett lifted his head and met my eyes. "I must be honest; I am really upset that you would choose to snoop around my store than to come to me with this."

His firm tone reminded me of Aunt Delia—a tone I rarely heard from my uncle.

"I feel like such a terrible person. I am sorry. You must believe me."

We locked eyes for several uncomfortable seconds, then his face relaxed. He nodded and gave a sympathetic smile. "I have to say," he said in a lighter tone. "I am relieved that we can now get this all out in the open. Even if it had to be under these circumstances."

Uncle Beckett sipped his tea and rubbed the back of his neck.

I sat quietly, stirring the now soggy frosted shredded wheat with my spoon.

"Your aunt had Andrew when she was eighteen."

My hands had become so sweaty, the spoon slipped from my fingers, clinked against the side of the bowl, and splattered milk on the counter. I quickly wiped it with my napkin. Even though I already knew this bit of information, it still seemed foreign coming from my uncle's mouth. Without any acknowledgement of my obvious nervous reaction, he continued.

"She became pregnant the summer after she graduated from high school. I wish I had known earlier because I could have helped."

"Who was he?"

"He, Adam Cole," my uncle paused, collecting his thoughts, "is my cousin."

"Your cousin? I don't understand."

"I wouldn't expect you to, Gwyn." He smiled slightly. "My parents raised Adam from the time he could walk. I thought of him as my little brother."

"Oh, so you knew about Andrew all these years?"

"Yes." Uncle Beckett nodded slightly, pursing his lips together.

"I can't believe you knew," I said, trying to hide a rising irritation that surprised me.

"I kept the secret because she asked me to." He reached across the counter and put his hand over mine. "Are you ready to hear the reason?"

I nodded.

"The spring of 1964, Adam turned 21. He was staying with my parents between tours in Vietnam at our vacation home along the coast. My parents thought it would be a good place for Adam to get his mind together. Like many young soldiers back then, he seemed so lost. That is, until he saw Delia."

Uncle Beckett spun the iced tea glass in a circle on the countertop.

"Adam met her at a bonfire. He called me the next day. I hadn't heard him that excited in a long time." Uncle Beckett paused and ran his finger down the glass, making a trail through the beaded condensation. "Gwyn, you may not realize this, but your aunt could have had any man she chose. Delia was beautiful."

"I've always thought she was pretty," I said.

Uncle Beckett pulled out one of the counter stools and sat down. He picked up an apple from the fruit basket, turned it over in his palm, and rubbed the stem with his thumb. He studied the apple skin as if it was a mirror. The peeled orange sat intact on a napkin.

"Delia broke off her engagement with a wealthy banker's son to be with Adam. The thought of telling her parents terrified her. She knew she would be disowned. Back then, many girls got engaged or even married right out of high school. Delia's parents had wanted her future to be set, but she didn't love him."

"I can't even imagine. How awful."

"Delia hid the pregnancy for as long as she could, but at a certain point—" Uncle Beckett shrugged. "It became hard to hide. They sent her to a maternity home in Pennsylvania. She was supposed to give up the baby and never look back."

"What about Adam? Did he ever know she was pregnant?" My heart raced, anticipating the answer.

"No, he never knew." Uncle Beckett ran his fingers through his hair and sighed. "Camp Holloway was attacked in February 1965, and Adam died. As soon as I heard, I called Delia's parents and searched for her. I'm not sure how I got it out of them, but they told me about her pregnancy. I went to the maternity home, but I was too late. Delia had already given birth, and the baby was gone.

"Thankfully, she hadn't left town yet. She had checked into a local motel. Instead of taking her back to her parents' house, I took her to mine. She talked about Adam, but never much about Andrew, and I never pressured her to."

Uncle Beckett removed his glasses and rubbed the corners of his eyes. "It was her idea to get married. We had both lost the loves of our lives. We were damaged. In a way, we understood each other like no one else could. She said we would survive just to spite the universe."

"That sounds like her," I said. "In those apocalypse movies, she would be the last one standing."

"Yes, she would." Uncle Beckett patted my hand. "Most couples say, 'I love you' when they leave for the workday, but in those early years, we said, 'Us against the world.'"

My aunt and uncle loved each other in their own way. It may not have been the traditional romance, but the relationship worked.

As a child, I never feared them breaking up, and that always comforted me.

Over the past few weeks, I only uncovered a fraction of what laid beneath my aunt's surface. She remained a fascinating mystery.

"Uncle, what about the trip to Italy and mom's rosary beads?" I asked.

"A lie, Gwyn. The beads were given to Delia from Sister Susan, a nun who attended at the maternity home in Popular Hill, Pennsylvania. I think Delia invented that story of Italy to let herself live a dream."

"Sister Susan sent the letters," I said with sudden realization. Sr. must be the abbreviation for Sister.

"She wasn't supposed to send Delia updates on Andrew," Uncle Beckett said. "Sister Susan broke rules to keep in touch, but I believe it was out of empathy for Delia. It was Sister Susan who told me where to find Delia, and I gave her my address to keep correspondence."

"I can't imagine living for over thirty years with a secret like that." I propped my elbow on the counter and pressed the weight of my forehead into my palm.

"The first couple years were awful for Delia," Uncle Beckett said. "She cried nearly every day. Then, one day, she stopped. She changed overnight; she lost the free-spirited personality and became disciplined, resolute. She never fell apart again—that is, until yesterday."

"And yesterday, she fell apart because of me."

"You can't blame yourself for this, Gwynnie." Uncle Beckett leaned across the counter and placed his hand on my shoulder. "Deep down, I knew she couldn't hold her pain inside forever. Even a rock eventually cracks."

"I had been seeing someone behind her back, and she found out," I said.

My uncle's left eyebrow shot up.

"A lot happened while you were gone," I said.

"I guess so." Uncle Beckett crossed his arms and smiled slyly. "Now, it seems it is your turn to talk."

31
SHIFTING SAND

*B*efore Isaac picked me up for the beach, I wrote a letter deferring my admission to Massachusetts College of Art and Design. I folded the letter neatly and placed the addressed envelope in my desk drawer to mail when I was ready. I had let Aunt Delia get to me, but this time, I didn't hate her for it.

DENISE FILLED her bright red bikini perfectly, and her flat stomach only accentuated her upper torso. I sat next to her on my Snoopy beach towel that I've had since the sixth grade. I still had on my white tank top over my bathing suit. Even though my bikini covered much more skin than Denise's, I was too self-conscious to remove it. I had always been uncomfortable in a bathing suit, whether I was seven, and embarrassed that my mom still made me wear a suit with ruffles across my rear end, or eighteen and self-conscious of my insignificant breasts.

I went to the beach all the time with my mom as a child. One time, during the summer I turned seven, Mom brought Jesse, one of her old boyfriends. They'd met at a gas station when he rushed out to pump her fuel even though she pulled in the self-serve bay. She could wear a burlap sack and still catch a man's eye. I remember thinking there was no way I wanted that much attention—after all, boys had cooties.

Denise turned toward me and dug her feet in the sand. "I can't believe we only have a few more weeks together."

"Me either. We've been together forever. I still have the BFF necklace we bought when we were ten." I propped my chin on my knees. "Remember, we saved up for them by selling lemonade?"

"I remember. I still have mine too." Denise smiled. "My dad likes to say the days are long, but the years are short. I think he's right."

"Yeah." I sighed. "You know what was long? Mr. Porter's Government class. If the Cold War wasn't boring enough?"

"And that opinion paper on NAFTA? Who makes high school seniors write about trade agreements?"

"I think Uncle Beckett practically wrote that one for me. He got a B."

Denise laughed. "Oh, I bet he was angry!"

"Yep," I said. "He was as glad for me to be done with that class as I was."

"I'll miss you, Gwyn Madison." Denise playfully shoved my leg.

"I'll miss you, too, Denise Prescott." I shoved her back. "But we'll see each other. We'll still talk."

My role had always been to be the serious friend. I found this sentimental version of Denise curious.

"Yeah, but it will be different," Denise said. "We'll be changing and growing in separate places. But that will give us new things to talk about."

I hadn't told Denise I planned to defer my enrollment for a year. Out of everyone, I thought she would be the most disappointed. She always called me her *smart friend*. Denise wanted me to leave this small town just as much as I thought I did.

"Every new beginning comes from some other beginning's end, right?" I said.

"Semisonic!" Denise said with a laugh. "Look at my smart friend making pop music references."

"Well, even if Semisonic ends up a one-hit wonder, I know we won't be." I put my arm around Denise and pulled her toward me until we both fell over.

"Come on, y'all, the water isn't too cold!" Danny yelled as he ran toward us. He held out his hand to Denise and pulled her onto her feet. He poked Denise against her bare side, and she giggled with childlike delight.

"Aren't you going swimming with us?" Danny shook his wet hair, sending a spray of droplets over my towel.

"I'm going to sit here and wait for Isaac to come back from the car."

"Suit yourself," Danny said.

He took off running, egging on Denise to chase him. They raced into the water. Denise managed to dunk Danny under the water, only to have him retaliate by doing the same.

I knelt on my beach towel, drawing circles in the sand with the edge of a broken shell. Maybe you should leave when things were good, so your last memory always brought happiness. I'd rather leave with a feeling of longing than a feeling of regret. Now, I just had to figure out which of those feelings was stronger.

A shadow of long legs moved over my primitive sand drawing.

"Where did your friends go?"

Shielding my eyes from the sun, I looked up at Isaac. "They went in the water. I told them I was waiting for you."

"Well, don't you want to go?"

I shrugged and tugged on the hem of my tank top to make sure it covered my midriff.

"Why not?"

"I don't want to get my clothes wet, that's all."

Isaac knelt in front of me. "Hey, that's silly. We're at the beach."

"I can't," I said, unable to look at him. "It's a stupid reason."

"Try me."

I pursed my lips, and I drew the word *no* in the sand.

"Come on. Whatever it is, I promise I won't laugh."

"Fine." I exhaled with such force that my bangs lifted, then fell back on my forehead. "I'm embarrassed, okay. Are you satisfied?"

"Embarrassed?" He turned my chin toward his smiling face. "Don't you know I already think you're beautiful?"

"Yes, but you've never seen me in a swimsuit." I laughed a little. I knew I sounded ridiculous.

"That's what you're worried about? When I couldn't find my swim trunks last night, my mom went out and bought these." Isaac gripped the hem of his trunks.

I bent down for a closer look. "Are those flamingos?"

"Yes, on surfboards. She still thinks I'm five." He pointed to his chest. "I'm the one who should be embarrassed."

"Okay, but I warn you, if you're totally grossed out, pretend otherwise."

"You could turn green, and I wouldn't care," Isaac said, then seemed to think about it. "Okay, maybe I would care about that."

"You're such a dork, but you're my dork." I lifted my tank top over my head and tossed it on a beach towel. The breeze gave me a chill, causing goosebumps to form on my arms. Isaac placed his hands on either side of my bare waist, and the goosebumps spread.

He leaned in and whispered, "I don't need to pretend."

Isaac kissed the edge of my jawline and worked his way to my mouth. His lips pressed against mine, and his hands inched their way up my side before stopping at my ribcage. Almost immediately, goosebumps formed from my calves to the base of my neck. At that moment, I knew how my aunt became lost in a boy she had only known a few months. I pulled away. Isaac's chest rose and fell in quick bursts; he was breathless too.

"Is everything okay?" He asked.

"It just got a little intense."

"Yeah, for me too." Isaac smiled, and his breathing slowed.

He held my hand as we listened to the waves break. A pelican took a nosedive into the ocean and then quickly rose with a fish dangling in his beak.

I squeezed his hand. "Maybe we should go in. They're probably wondering what's taking us so long."

32
PEACE

It's never too late to be who you might have been. —George Eliot

The strong smell of oregano, which belonged to Brenda's leftovers heating in the oven, filled Aunt Delia's kitchen. Isaac set the beach bag down by the pantry door. A stream of sand oozed from a small hole in the bottom corner of the blue canvas. Normally, I would have rushed to clean up such a mess, but this time, I figured it could wait.

We followed the voices of my mom and Serena to the far side of the house. They were standing outside of Aunt Delia's closed bedroom door.

Mom moved in for a hug. "Hey, baby, I'm glad you guys made it home safely. Did you have fun?"

"We did." Isaac reached out to shake her hand. "It's nice to see you again."

"So polite," Mom said.

"I explained to Trisha the pain medication your aunt is on," Serena said. "We might make her a nurse yet."

Serena winked at me and handed Mom a clipboard with several pages of instructions.

"That would be good," I said. "I've been telling her she should do it for years."

I smiled at my mom. She covered her face with the clipboard so I wouldn't see her blush.

"Listen to your daughter, Trisha. She's a smart one."

"I know she is," Mom said, sounding proud. "My daughter's going to be a college grad someday."

A knot formed in my stomach as I began to mentally reread the letter I had written that morning.

"Your aunt wanted to see you," Serena said. "Go on in."

I turned the doorknob and glanced over my shoulder as Serena mouthed something to Isaac, which he acknowledged with a nod. He grabbed my free hand and followed me into the bedroom.

The lights were off, and the window shades were pulled to allow only about eight inches of light to spill in on either side of my aunt's bed. The heavy scents of lavender and muscle cream enveloped the room.

"Aunt Delia..." I paused and breathed deeply. "This is Isaac."

I placed my hand lightly on Isaac's shoulder.

Isaac nodded at my aunt, and she returned the gesture in a way that made me feel as if they already knew each other. I threw him a glance, but he only smiled at me. Serena's silent words, Aunt Delia's overly familiar nod—something strange was happening.

"Isaac," she said softly, "I need to speak to my niece alone. I hope you don't mind."

"I don't mind at all, ma'am," Isaac said. "I'll wait for you outside."

Aunt Delia waited to speak until Isaac had closed the door.

"Come here, Gwyn." She patted the bed quilt with her hand. Aunt Delia's tone was considerably composed compared to when I spoke with her in the hospital.

"Uncle Beckett told me the story about Andrew and how Adam died," I said. "I am so sorry. That must have been so horrible."

Andrew's name was becoming to me as familiar as my own. I had recently started to imagine what he might look like. I wondered if he had blue eyes like me and his mom.

"I did not want to speak to you about my past." Aunt Delia tried to push herself upright in the bed but winced in pain and gave up, falling back into the pillows. She took a deep breath. "I wanted to talk about your future."

"Oh," I said quietly.

"What is this I hear about you wanting to defer this semester?"

"How did you find that out? I only told Isaac."

I tapped my forehead with my fingers. Isaac. He was thirty minutes late picking me up this morning.

"He visited me in the hospital early this morning."

I pursed my lips. "He shouldn't have told you, Aunt Delia. This was my decision to make."

"You should not be angry with him," she said as if reading my thoughts. "He did the right thing. When we see those we love about to make a huge mistake, it's human nature to want to intervene."

"I'm confused. I thought you would be happy about my decision to defer."

I couldn't look my aunt in the eyes because I didn't want to cry. Instead, I fixed my eyes on a bluebird perched on the feeder outside the window. At that moment, I would have gladly changed places with him.

"No, I agree with Isaac," Aunt Delia said emphatically.

"What?" I asked in astonishment. The bird quickly flew away as if my shock startled him.

"Yes, you need to go."

"But why, Aunt Delia? I told Isaac I needed to stay here and help you."

"Taking care of me is not your responsibility."

"But this whole thing is my fault. The lies, your accident—"

My aunt held up her hush finger, a signal to stop talking.

"Young lady, do not think you alone hold the market on lies? As of today, I am done with secrets. Look at me, Gwyn," she said firmly.

The pain medication must have been doing its job because she suddenly seemed back to normal. "Do you know where the money came from? The money I was saving to send you to college?"

I shook my head.

"My parents and I did not speak for a long time after I married

Beckett," she said. "And then you were born and changed everything. I wanted to make sure you had the opportunity that I didn't, so I asked my parents for the money that was intended for me, to save for you. And I've been saving ever since."

"You did that for me?"

"Everything I have done has been for you. I realize now that I should have given you more freedom. I thought that restriction would guarantee you had the opportunity. I was afraid, and I was wrong. And I am very sorry I never said I was proud of you."

Sorry hung in the room like the air after a southern mid-winter snowfall, both unexpected and welcomed. The one word I had never heard my aunt say. The one word I needed to hear most of all.

I couldn't speak.

"That boy in there—" She raised her hand a few inches off the quilt to point in the direction of the door. "He loves you. No one has ever fought for me like that. And when he came to speak to me on your behalf, I had to listen." Her tone lightened. "He's a breath of fresh air. Let's face it, no one else in my family has the guts to stand up to me."

I couldn't help but smile at my aunt's wit, thankful her sharp personality wasn't entirely shaken away by the accident. Her labored breathing contrasted the stillness of the summer's evening. A breeze moved the sheer curtains. I found it strange that I hadn't noticed the windows were ajar. I had been in the room for at least fifteen minutes. My gaze followed a ladybug as she pulled herself over the window ledge and disappeared. A sudden feeling of peace passed through me.

"So, you're letting me go," I said softly.

"Yes, dear, I'm letting you go."

33
SETTLING SUMMER

"I can't believe you're leaving, Gwyn," Denise said as she threw her arms around me, pressing her head against my collarbone. I squeezed back.

"Yeah, and you better not come home with some crazy accent," Danny teased before giving my hair a brotherly tousle and sandwiching both of us in a hug.

"I'll miss you guys, too, but right now I can't breathe." I tilted my chin upward to give my nostrils air. My friends released me and laughed.

"You always were a lightweight," Danny said, punching me in the shoulder.

"Oww." I smirked as I shook my tingling arm.

Isaac crossed my front yard with my duffle bag and a crate of books. My friends turned in the direction of my gaze.

"Hey, Danny." Denise patted Danny on the chest. "Let's give them some privacy. We can go in and see if Uncle Beck needs some help."

Danny fist-bumped Isaac's shoulder as they passed on the lawn.

"Don't you know any other way to greet someone?" Isaac asked, before breaking into a wide smile.

Danny shrugged. "At least I make an impression." He bowed and tipped an invisible top hat.

The remaining short weeks of summer had passed in a blur. The household quickly fell into a routine of working, cooking, and caring for Aunt Delia. The doctors cleared her to go back to work in a week, and I knew she was counting down the hours. Isaac visited practically every day and so did Brenda. As the morning finally arrived that Uncle Beckett would drive me to Boston, it almost seemed as if the anger and hurt I experienced earlier in the summer was now a distant memory. Amazing what three months could do.

"Earth to Gwyn," Isaac said as he snapped his fingers in front of my face. I blinked, suddenly aware of his presence. "Where were you just now?"

"Thinking. So much has happened this summer." I reached out and pulled him toward me.

"God, I'm going to miss you." He tucked a stray hair behind my ear. I shivered. His touch still gave me chills. The handle of the passenger door of Uncle Beckett's Chrysler pressed into my lower back, but I didn't care. I wanted to make this moment last. I closed my eyes as I traced his jawline with my fingers.

"Don't worry," Isaac whispered. "Remember, we're only—"

"A train ride away," I said, finishing his sentence.

"That's right."

"And I'll be there, my fall break in D.C.," I said.

"And my birthday in Boston." Isaac reached down and picked up the New England guidebook, which he had given me for my birthday, from the crate. He flipped through the pages. "I noticed you had tabbed each place I listed with a Post-It note."

"We were going to check them off one-by-one, remember?"

"Yes, that's the plan."

I turned toward the Volvo packed with all my worldly possessions, then to my childhood home. I wanted to take it all in. I felt my back pocket for the graduation present from Dad, a hundred-dollar BP gift card. Even though I didn't see Dad often, he looked out for me in his own way. Dad said since he couldn't drive me to college, he still wanted to help me get there.

Sometimes I doubted that I deserved the chances I'd been given, but I would do my best to make those chances mean something. I surveyed the yard and watched everyone moving about. This is what I would miss about home, all the moments that look mundane to an outside observer but mean everything to the person at the center. Danny carried boxes from the garage, while Mom showed Brenda the rose bush Charlie helped her plant outside of Aunt Delia's favorite window. Mrs. Jenkins waved as she stepped out of her car, and Uncle Beckett walked over to greet her. And then there was Denise writing the words *College Bound* on the back windshield of the car. Isaac interlaced his fingers in mine.

These were my people, and I loved them. I thought that maybe next summer, there would be one more person standing in the front yard. A person who may look a little like me, a person I never knew I missed before this summer. I closed my eyes and pictured myself walking into my first college art class, the classroom heavy with the smell of oil paints, as Aunt Delia searched for Andrew for the very first time.

WHISPERING THROUGH WATER READER'S GUIDE

Are you ready for more of Whispering Through Water? Check out the Monarch website www.monarcheducationalservices.com for the Whispering Through Water Reader's Guide. This free educational resource is perfect for educators, librarians, homeschools, small groups, and readers who want more of Gwyn's story.

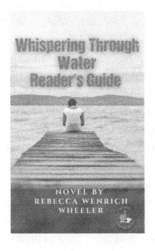

AUTHOR'S NOTE

Whispering Through Water could not have been set in the modern age of smartphones and DNA testing, when long-held secrets can be revealed with a swipe of a mouth swab and an Internet search. I first became interested in the stories of women who were forced to surrender babies for adoption when I heard an NPR interview of Ann Fessler discussing her book *The Girls Who Went Away: The Hidden History of Women Who Surrendered Children for Adoption in the Decades Before Roe v. Wade* (2006). I immediately bought a copy of the book. It was an emotional read. One that I had to read in small chunks, but then couldn't put it down. In the two decades prior to 1973, an estimated 1.5 million American women were forced to give up children for adoption. These births happened under a veil of secrecy so as to not bring shame to the family. Pregnant and unwed, the women were often forced to drop out of school or lose their jobs if they kept their babies. The mothers were told they would in time forget about what happened to them, but how do you go about forgetting? Many of these birth mothers will never be able to speak their own truth, as their secrets have passed away with them. With the rising use of DNA testing to map genealogy, undoubtedly more people will learn of this tragic time in our country's history. These forced separations affected the trajectory of a person's life generations later, both for the mother and the child. Approach these stories with empathy because empathy is the catalyst for change.

ACKNOWLEDGMENTS

When I was about eleven, my mom gave me a copy of *Silas Marner*, which had been her favorite book as a youth. She told me that George Eliot was a woman, and she had to write under a man's name to be taken seriously. I am grateful that is not a choice I am forced to make. Thank you to the women who persisted before us, and may our granddaughters never know the feeling of being stifled. To my Grandma Helen who gave me lots of books and taught me age was just a number, and to my parents who taught me that every day was a good day to learn something new. My sister, thanks for always showing up. To Ray Lingle and Shahgol Mostashari, who lived through 1998 with me, as the Kenny and Dolly duet says, "You Can't Make Old Friends". To Tonya Hinton, who I met as a grown up, and I can't imagine surviving life without. Jessica Fowler, thanks for being my cheerleader, and Terri Moore for your art and enduring support. To Jen Lowry, mere words will never be enough, but thank you for your faith in me. To my Monarch Press editors, you help me clean up well. My children, Helen and Xander, you make me a better person just by your existence, and Sam, you were it from the beginning. And finally, to my senior English teacher Patricia Hoppe and college English professor Dr. Cordelia Hanneman, you not only taught me the value of a comma, but to believe in the power of my own words.

ABOUT THE AUTHOR

Rebecca Wenrich Wheeler was raised in West Point, a small town in the Tidewater region of Virginia. From the moment she submitted her first short story to a young author's contest in second grade, Rebecca knew she wanted to be a writer. Her love of writing led her to earn a BA in English and an MEd in English education. She spent several years as a high school teacher, during which she also developed a passion for mental health advocacy. Rebecca completed an MA in professional counseling and now serves as an elementary school counselor and college adjunct psychology instructor. Rebecca teaches yoga for the young and the young at heart, and she likes to infuse yoga and breathwork in her counseling practice wherever she can. She believes the most valuable use of her time is teaching youth how to love and care for each other and the world around them. Her stories share this focus on positive relationships and a love of nature. Rebecca now lives in Durham, North Carolina, with her husband, two children, and two spoiled Siamese cats.

If you know someone is hurting or if that person is you, please reach out. Talk to school staff, family, and/or a friend, and reach out for professional help if needed. Know you are not alone. You are loved.

National Suicide Prevention Lifeline: 988
Crisis Text Line: Text "Hello" to 741741
National Alliance on Mental Illness (NAMI) www.nami.org
National Center for PTSD: www.ptsd.va.gov/

CPSIA information can be obtained
at www.ICGtesting.com
Printed in the USA
BVHW072136130123
656272BV00007B/302